THE WORKERS

BOOKS BY AUDREY LEE

THE CLARION PEOPLE

THE WORKERS

THE
WORKERS

BY AUDREY LEE

McGRAW-HILL BOOK COMPANY

NEW YORK ST. LOUIS SAN FRANCISCO

LONDON SYDNEY TORONTO

MEXICO PANAMA

The characters set down in *The Workers* are
entirely fictional.
If they resemble persons either living or dead,
the resemblance is a coincidence.

THE WORKERS

Library of Congress Catalog Card Number: 76-81609

First Edition

36991

FOR KENNETH

CHAPTER

1

Harvie Guthrie waiting at the traffic light, his whole being wavering between alternatives. Stop. Go. The glowing, yellow-face clock over the City Hall mechanically striking down the hours. Five. Soaring to keep abreast of the era of rampant innovation and murder. The weight of his plight settling upon him now that he has stepped into the December air. Fired from his job on Christmas Eve.

The icy wind screaming, move on.

So vulnerable is the spirit seeking attunement with an inconstant age.

Harvie at the newsstand. Shall he buy the *Daily News, Bulletin,* or *Inquirer?* Which paper has more want advertisements? Which offers the best jobs? Dare he scan the want advertisment section on the street where everyone will know he is without a job, that he is a failure?

He has his severance pay. But he cannot rejoice. The rent is due, the telephone, gas. He must find another job. Harvie afraid of the possibility that inside him lie unpredictable forces of which he is unaware.

Certainly he never intended to dash that new adding machine

1

against the floor. But he did—simply because he could not apply his dexterity to the new machine. It minimized the importance of his dexterity.

Harvie shuddering at the crash of the machine resounding in his memory, thinking that thereafter the fitting thing for him to have done was to rave, thereby justifying his unpremeditated action. Everything was static until he created the drama, the catharsis for his dormant condition, until he startled his co-workers, caused all their eyes to turn on him, until he interrupted the fixed routine.

He was used to the old machine. How his hands did fly over the keys. How well he knew their identity with a single instinctive touch. His fingers deftly prodded the keys for answers.

The hands prod on, the body commended to its static station. Harvie thinking that communication offers accord, offers dialogue of a kind. He can still see Mr. Davidson, the office manager, leaning forward in the great chair behind the great desk within the panelled walls decorated with seascapes, portraits of his wife and children, and the drapery-covered windows reflecting a field of commercial buildings emitting white streamers of smoke. He can still hear his voice.

"You're not flexible, Guthrie. To get on, you must be flexible. Machines are changing. They're faster and they're more efficient. You have to adapt yourself to the changes. The machine does the work, but you're the man in charge. Understand what I'm trying to say, Guthrie—for the future. I'm going to have to let you go."

Harvie turning his thoughts away from Davidson & Davidson, having decided upon a newspaper.

"Inquirer, please."

He is searching the want advertisement section over coffee in The Cafeteria. Harvie drinking the last of his coffee. He has found something, circling the advertisement on the Classified page, fifth row:

Competent Adding Machine Operator.
Dexterous. Temporary Assignment.
Hours Flexible.

Looking up from his paper at the thick hands removing his empty cup and saucer, putting them on the cart filled with dirty dishes. An elderly woman marked with a curvature of the spine, feet encased in corrective shoes.

Harvie thinking: Does she like her job or doesn't she think about the work she does? Does she like collecting dirty cup after dirty cup, saucer, plate, scraping the garbage? Is she compensated for the unpleasantness, as well as for the performance of the job? Has she ever become angry and dashed a tray onto the floor? Of course not.

Her brief smile reminds Harvie that he is staring at her. Harvie moving his hands so that she can apply the damp cloth to the table. She wiping once, twice, done; moving on, methodically, collecting plates, cups, silverware, swiping the tables with the cloth.

He doesn't imagine that she has a voice, that she ever says anything. She is a worker and she works. She looking as if she has been created solely for the purpose of work, as if she should have no reason for existing other than to clear the tables of other people's crumbs, dirty silver, dishes. She looking as if she has worked in The Cafeteria ever since she was born. When she dies, her hands will move on, her feet. How many miles?

She wears no ornaments, not even a watch, having no need of time. What would she do with time, Harvie thinking, watching the slow movement of her corrective shoes designed for the miles she will walk today, tomorrow. How many miles? Don't ask questions. Move on, Harvie Guthrie.

He will apply for the temporary job. But there is something precarious about working this way. No guarantee of his working every day. But Harvie Guthrie is at loose ends, total job insecurity being part of it. He must work, even if he does not have work every day.

A traffic policeman blowing his whistle, telling a motorist to move on. A pigeon lighting on the curb, holding a bread crumb in its beak with something of reserve. Flying away with the fare still in its beak.

Harvie staring at the ground, looking up to see several people staring too, trying to see what he sees. Already idleness is making him feel eccentric.

Harvie feeling embarrassed, walking away without looking back, thinking that Mr. Davidson should have considered the value of his dexterity before firing him. Surely, human dexterity is important over every machine. Then, too, hadn't Harvie faithfully worked in Accounting for seven years? Mrs. Long, Mr. Davidson's secretary, had praised Harvie's dexterity, but she criticised his being so quiet. He never joined in, she said. One never knew about quiet people like him. Still water ran deep, as the saying went.

Harvie drifting among the clusters of Christmas shoppers bearing gaudy Christmas shopping bags, boxes, and crossing the street from every direction. Harvie listening to recorded Christmas carols competing with the din of automibile horns and churning motors. Turning toward the familiar rattle of the mechanical toy soldier marking time in the open window of the novelty shop. He will miss passing the window in which the toy has marched for at least a month. Harvie watching the mechanical toy jump up and down like a thing seemingly obsessed with motion.

"Intriguing, isn't it, friend?"

Harvie turning toward the unshaven, smiling, large-framed man looking over his shoulder, feeling intruded upon.

"It runs on batteries," bending his unshaven head to get a closer look. "My name's Hardy Gallant."

"If you're looking for a handout, you've come to the *wrong* man. I haven't got a job either."

"I knew we had something in common, friend," extending a hand. "Come, friend. There's nothing in my hand but my palm. And, of course, a sense of touch. My name's Hardy Gallant. The most significant thing about me is that I named myself. Now, what's yours?"

"Harvie Guthrie."

"Harvie Guthrie, is it? Your name may be part of your trouble. There's a connection."

"Connection?"

"Yes. There's a connection between your name and your circumstance. *Harvie Guthrie*. Now, what kind of name is *that?* You hear it and right away you think: He's a loser."

"I didn't name myself."

"What kind of work do you do, Guthrie?"

"I worked in the Accounting Department. They took my machine."

"Well, don't sound so broken about it. You'd think they took your wife. You married, Harvie?"

"No."

"Well then, why do you *have* to work? You're a thinking man. A thinking man avoids work contrary to his thinking. Don't you know when you're *free?*

"Or would you rather be like that toy—jumping all the time? Some people go through their lives jumping like that. They never relax long enough to enjoy a holiday. Where do you live, Harvie?"

"Uptown."

"Get rid of it, Guthrie. It's a hindrance. It's an obligation. What does it mean—this uptown, huh? It means that you have to work harder to stay there. Look at you. You're in a panic—not because you don't have a job, but because you have that uptown place and you won't be able to pay the rent. Give it up, Harvie, and you'll be free. Do you smell the evergreen? Do you smell the holly?"

"What's that got to do with it?"

"Do you think you'd be smelling it if you were one of those people? Look at them. Risking their lives just to get to the other side of the street to spend their money. You're free. You've got no money to risk your life for. You can live your life slow and easy.

"You and I are philosophers, Harvie. You don't need your machine. What have machines to say to men like us, huh? We communicate with people. Watch.

"Merry Christmas, madam. Looks like you've got an armful. Toys for the kiddies?"

"Yes. How did you know?"

"You look like a thoughtful grandmother, that's how I know, madam. I can always tell when a person cares about her fellow man. She wears it."

"Is that so? Thank you."

"May I ask you a question? You can say no, if you want to."

"Yes, of course."

"I *knew* you'd say yes. A dollar would be too much. All I need is fifty cents. It would give me a place to sleep this Christmas Eve, and I'd be able to celebrate Christmas Day. Thank you, madam. Thank you. You didn't have to give me a whole dollar. Merry Christmas, madam. And many more!"

"Merry Christmas to you, too."

"You did that as if you were used to doing that kind of thing, Gallant. It's not the kind of practice you can continue without getting into trouble. You're not the weakest, most dependent-looking man I've seen. A longshoreman couldn't look any healthier. Somebody's going to tell you to get a job."

"Harvie, Harvie. If I didn't know we were friends, I'd think you were trying to insult me. Now watch this.

"Sir. Pardon me, sir—for interrupting your line of thought. You were thinking about the gift in the box you're carrying. For a woman, sir. A very *special* woman."

"How did you know?"

"I can tell. You wear it in your expression. And you're a gambling man. You're not sure she'll accept, but you bought it anyway. You believe in your ability to *persuade*. You are a professional businessman."

"Yes, of course."

"You're wondering how I can tell. Your distinctive manner, your confidence. It sets you apart."

"Thank you."

"Now, if I tell you where you got that gift for the worthy lady, would it be worth a dollar to you—being the gambling man that you are—if I'm wrong?"

"Where *did* I get it?"

"You got it under your arm."

"That's pretty good. Pretty good! Five shouldn't do you any harm on Christmas Eve."

"Thank you, sir. Every success with the lady."

"Thank you."

"Brilliant, don't you agree, Harvie? You get to them when they're feeling good, when they have a good opinion of themselves. That's when they're most generous. Now he's going to celebrate his generosity and buy something for himself."

"You guess."

"I *know*. He'll be talking about the poor beggar he gave five dollars to until next Christmas. You try somebody. It's the season for conscience."

"No thanks!" thrusting his hands into his pockets, dallying among the flow of people, the rattle of shopping bags, recorded voices caroling. Hark the herald angels.

"What you need is touch, Harvie. You're out of touch. You've been working with machines too long, Harvie. Watch me again.

"Howdy, madam. You don't remember me from last Christmas. The dollar you gave generously. If I had a hat, I'd take it off to you. It was the merriest Christmas I ever had."

"Why, yes, young man. How are things going for you now?"

"About the same, madam. Even a strong man can have trouble getting to his feet."

"I'm sorry to hear that. I'm always glad to help people who help themselves."

"*Five dollars.* Madam! You *shouldn't* have. How can I ever repay you?"

"Continue going to college. And buy that hat."

"Thank you. If I had a hat, I'd take it off to you."

"You didn't tell me you were going to college, Gallant."

"I'm not going to college, Harvie. And I never saw her before. She's never seen me. Didn't you see the surprise on her face?"

"No. I didn't see it."

"It's like I told you. You have to keep in touch, bring the generosity out of people."

"Couldn't you get arrested for that?"

"*Arrested?* For bringing the generosity out of people? *Harvie!* It's my *work*. You work with machines and I work with people. You get the best from machines. I get the best from people. You surprise me, asking a question like that. Both of us are concerned about the need for generous people.

"Look at the ordinary man who stands with his hat out, the nonprofessional. If there's one coin in his hat, somebody will come along and throw another to match the one already there. But if the man is smart, he won't let too many coins accumulate. He'll put most of them in his pocket. Why? Because if he's got a hatful of coins people will think he's got enough, that he ought to be thankful and go home.

"If his hat is empty, nobody wants to put anything in it. They're suspicious. There must be a good reason why nobody else has given the poor man a coin. And they can pass him with a good conscience."

"You know a lot about people, don't you?"

"A conscience usually does. Are you going to stand in this spot all night and let that mechanical toy hypnotize you, or do you want to see what the rest of the world is like?"

"*A large shopping bag. Fifteen cents. Large shopping bag. Fifteen cents.*"

"What fair lady are we happening upon, Guthrie? Selling shopping bags, the beautiful creature. Hark, I will speak to her to make certain that she is real. Hello, beautiful. My friend and I sure would like to put you into one of those shopping bags and take you home. She doth not respond, Guthrie. See what I mean? Even a man's greeting a strange woman inspires in her a good opinion of herself. I've flattered her into thinking that she is too important to return the greeting to an *ordinary* man like me. Oh, well, it's Christmas, Harvie. What do you know? You play the harmonica."

"How do you know?"

"I'm in touch. Besides, you have one in your pocket. Look, sometimes you have to give cheer in order to get it, right? You play one note on your harmonica, then another, until you're playing a song. You finish that song and you've got the feeling for music. What a man needs is expression. If he keeps things bottled up inside he stifles.

"Here's a cheerful spot. Christmas lights are good backdrop. Christmas tree, toys, and the Nativity scene. And we certainly aren't at a loss for people."

"What are you about this time, Gallant?"

"We're going to make music, Harvie, of course. You're going to play the harmonica and I'm going to sing."

"Oh, no, we're not."

"Don't tell me you lack the courage to make music. Guthrie. What are you coming to? Since when does it take guts to make music? That's all you'll be doing is making music. If people want to express themselves and their appreciation for our music by giving us a donation, don't protest and don't stop playing. Everybody needs to express himself. We'll sing this one first: *DA DA DA da da da DA DA DA. Da da da da da da da da da, DA DA DA DA.*

"*God bless you, gentlemen. God bless you. If you haven't got a ha' penny, well, God bless you!. . .*"

CHAPTER

2

"You make good music, Guthrie. Nothing like the spirit of Christmas. Have another beer. Remember the Infant Christ wrapped in swaddling clothes and laid in a manger because there was no room at the inn—and He was worthy. With me, Guthrie, it was just a bad break. I gave up my job over truth."

"Truth?"

"Yes. Have another beer."

"Thanks, I think I will. I think I will have another beer. You're a real sport to cheer me like this, Gallant. Nobody sympathizes with a loser. You're a real friend."

"We've come to the right place for cheers, Guthrie."

"I've been thinking, Gallant—"

"Thinking?"

"People aren't as real as they used to be. They're afraid of a natural thing like a smile. They're afraid that if they smile, they've committed themselves. You walked up to me when I was looking at that mechanical toy, and I thought you wanted something from me. Instead, you're giving *me* something."

"It's nothing, Guthrie. Christmas spirit. Have another beer."

"Thanks, friend. You know, I liked that old machine."

10

"Never mind the machine, Guthrie. Drink your beer."

"Why don't you let him take the empty bottles?"

"I want to keep count."

"How many bottles so far, Gallant?"

"Eight, Guthrie. Who drank all that beer? Barkeep!"

"If you think we shouldn't—"

"And miss all that Christmas spirit, Guthrie? *Barkeep!*"

"A while ago you were saying—"

"Saying what, Guthrie?"

"About leaving your job because of truth—"

"Oh—*truth*. Truth hasn't changed, Guthrie. That's why it's truth. There's got to be room for people like us, but what can we expect, if there was no room in the inn for Christ?"

"You don't know how grateful I am to have somebody to talk to. I've never felt so relaxed."

"Have another beer, Guthrie."

"You were going to tell me about truth."

"I don't have to tell you about truth, Guthrie. It's yours to know. It depends on which way you travel. And you have to ask yourself if you're ready for truth."

"You ought to come with me, Guthrie. Rent's cheaper. It makes it easy to concentrate on truth because you don't have to worry about that uptown place. You have fifty cents?"

"Is that all it costs, fifty cents?"

"For a bed. Coffee is extra. But if you want to look around first—"

"I don't think I want to live that far down—with all due respect to your suggestion, of course."

"I understand. If you can afford to live *better*."

"No. It's not that. I expect to get another job soon."

"Look at you. You can't enjoy your freedom even for a few hours. Now, Harvie, when have you sat down on a work evening and drunk bottles and bottles of beer without having to think about going to work the next day?"

"You're angry."

"I'm not angry. Have another beer."

"I'm afraid, Gallant."

"You're afraid? Of what?"

"If I don't get another job right away, I'll lose my dexterity."

"Your *what?*"

"My dexterity. I'm very good with the adding machine."

"Oh, *that*. I know what you mean. Watch the bottle, Harvie. I'll be back."

"I'll wait right here." Looking after Hardy Gallant easing sideways through the maze of men standing behind others seated at the bar, easing through the thick wall of smoke and the strong scent of beer. The men laughing at the man wavering on the bar stool at the farther end of the bar.

"*Water?* Did you say water? Who needs water? I asked you for brandy."

"I can't serve you any more liquor. You're drunk."

"You served me before. And who says I'm drunk? I'm drunk when I cannot ask for anything more to drink. I'm drunk when I cannot see you—you are there. And there are the bottles. All it takes is one bottle to send me where I want to be. You have the power to lift your fellow man. Look at them. Bottles and bottles and bottles. Is it the bottle you're worried about? I only want what's in it. You can have the bottle back. How's that?"

"No."

"I know—you're a smart one. You don't trust me. You're afraid I might drink the bottle. All right. I'll make a bargain. I'll give you a deposit on the bottle. If I don't give it back, you can keep the deposit."

"Go home and get some sleep, Champ."

"A second thought, barkeep. Give me just one little drink for my travels, something that will send me straight home."

"I'm sorry. . . ."

"*He's* sorry. All right, barkeep. Give a man who's unsteady on his feet a hand. Thank you. You're a gentleman. Good night."

"Hello, Guthrie. I'm back. Looks like that fellow had his fill. Look at him go. Are you feeling your beers, yet, Harvie?"

"I feel *all right*, if that's what you mean."

"You have some color in your face, at least. I bought you a present."

"What is it?"

"Who is the person you hate most of all?"

"Davidson. He fired me, didn't he? He's a—"

"Don't say it, Guthrie. I know how you feel. It's a representation of Davidson, sure enough."

"Open the box and let me at him!"

"Sure, Guthrie. One punishment deserves another. There. I ordered the man to give me the one in the window. This one seems more like your Davidson. You want to wind him up?"

"The toy soldier. For me? Gallant, you shouldn't have."

"I didn't know you'd be so touched."

"You wind him. I might bust him. I want him to know what it's like to be tortured first."

"Sure, Guthrie. Meanwhile, let's have another beer," winding the toy. The mechanical legs jerking up and down, marking time. Hardy Gallant bending over the toy. "Now, Davidson, you recognize Harvie Guthrie as the man you fired. Now we're going to make you sweat. March, Davidson! You—"

"Now, Gallant, I thought you didn't like profane language."

"I lost my head, Guthrie. Listen, Guthrie, it's getting late. I have to find someplace to sleep tonight."

"If I didn't live so far uptown, Gallant, I'd invite you to—"

"I know how it is, Guthrie. Thanks for thinking of me. Let's drink this last beer to something. What do we drink to, Guthrie?" Pushing a black wave of hair from his forehead. "Let's drink to truth. To truth." Lifting his glass. "Tomorrow, truth."

"Why is it always tomorrow, Gallant?"

"It's marked that way on the calendar. You have to keep in touch, Guthrie. Maybe we'll meet again. Whenever you feel like bumming."

"You're a real friend, Gallant. Cheers, whether we meet again or not."

"Cheers to you too, Guthrie."

Harvie Guthrie pacing the floor of his uptown place. Dance, Harvie Guthrie, and change the pace. In the living room, in the bedroom, back to the living room. Sitting on the sofa, on the bed.

Harvie Guthrie stifling with energy, gifted with dexterity, confined in limiting space. Shall he huff and puff and blow the house down? Who will put the house together again? Harvie Guthrie is not a builder. He is a worker who needs work.

What were the things he used to think of doing if he didn't have to work? He can think of none. He must get out of the apartment, move in space, find his niche. He has never been in the apartment so early in the day. Harvie Guthrie is used to evening shadows.

Harvie Guthrie at the mailbox. The gas bill, the electric bill, the rent, the Eternal Revenue—rather, the Internal Revenue. Climbing the stairs, putting the bills aside, lying on the sofa, immobilized, closing his eyes. Sleep, Harvie Guthrie, beyond care.

3

The sound of work-bound feet clicking and scraping the ground. Every day Harvie has heard those sounds upon the walk, never having listened because he was part of the sound, always in step. He has no job now, Harvie feeling out of step. Stopping at the bus stop, watching the swinging, braceleted arms, the attaché-laden hands of the workers whose efforts will effect progress, their own potential for personal progress remaining static.

All of the men and women rushing to work. The window washers have already begun their work on the shop windows, the windows smearing, tearing, clearing. The clock on the City Hall striking nine. The janitors sweeping the pavements, or having swept, now leaning upon their brooms, spitting the dust from their lungs.

The bank tellers readying themselves for the day's intake, output. The stock market, pulse of the nation's pulse, ticking. Philadelphia, New York, Washington Stock Exchange, Dow-Jones Average.

The man crouching in stocking feet arranging clothing in the display window. The doors of the department stores revolving round and round. Window displays of women's wear, men's wear,

15

furniture, household appliances; gadgets for the woman, for the man who has everything. The counters abundant with handkerchiefs, handbags, cosmetics, shirts, blouses. The salesladies, salesmen waiting to serve.

Excavators breaking the street, the excavation area cordoned off with barricades and red flags.

A Negro boy shining a sailor's shoes, snapping the shoeshine cloth, bringing up the shine, switching two brushes from hand to hand.

The traffic policemen blowing his whistle, waving the automobiles on.

A blind man offering his cup to the flurry of footsteps, simultaneously stroking the back of his seeing-eye dog sprawled on the ground beside him, the dog yawning and flexing its ears.

A man in a wheelchair slobbering like a baby, holding a tin cup between his blanket-covered knees, his hands moving vaguely. Watching a man whom he recognizes coming toward him. The man partially removing the blanket covering his crippled legs. Releasing a metal clamp on a rubber tube, placing the tube into a urinal. The man in the wheelchair uttering a yawnlike sound. The other man responding with a smile and a nod and waving goodbye.

The steam of myriad breaths on the noon air of the workers rushing. The derelicts charming, disarming.

"Madam. You wouldn't believe the tragedy that befalls a man. Still, God is good to us." Hardy Gallant. "I wouldn't be standing here, if He weren't. Madam, I just wouldn't be alive, the trouble I've seen, if it weren't for the good Lord. I just buried my mother and my father died last week, and I'm up to my elbows in debt. And there's nobody left but me on this earth." Hardy Gallant keeping in step with her quick, short paces, pointing to the bar on the opposite side of the street. "Could you not spare me one small quarter so that I can go over there and smile—for just a minute or two—thank you, madam. You're a practicing Christian woman. For every goodness you do, madam, you receive that many more in Heaven."

"Sir."

"Yes. I know. You buried your mother. I heard. This ought to buy a guffaw."

"Thank you, sir, for being so perceptive of a poor man's problems. You're storing your treasures in Heaven," rushing across the street to the saloon.

The stoplight, the people converging, merging.

Harvie Guthrie boarding the bus, riding several blocks, rising to get off, hesitating at the exit, the bus rolling on. Searching his pockets for the advertisement. *Competent adding machine operator. Dexterous.* Having once decided to apply for the job, he is now undecided. Exercising his fingers, hands, listening to the joints cracking. Winter stiffens the joints and idleness robs hands of their dexterity.

The end of the bus line. Harvie standing at the land's edge, looking over the water, the horizon vaguely visible behind a veil of mist. Sink or swim. Does Harvie want to swim? Swim toward *what?* Toward some veiled horizon? Sink or swim. What alternatives? *Either. Or.*

The ice-blue air growling. Move on, Harvie Guthrie. Here things move on. Out. Beyond. Here sea captains anchor. Longshoremen unload cargo channeled to port by sea captains' ships. The wind snarling. Move on.

This is no place for dreaming. The water is muddy. Rotten logs float. Discarded anchors stick in the mud, scum mildew, fungus, the muted rainbow of stagnant water. The brash baritone of a ship's horn. Moving out. Harvie lighting a cigarette, moving on.

The bus returning. The end of the line is now the beginning. Flicking the cigarette into the air. Boom. It lands, splintering sparks upon the cold street. The wind growling. Move on.

The clock on the City Hall striking one. What will Harvie do? Apply for the job? Idleness has disturbed his habits, left him unsettled. He used to get up at six o'clock each morning. He was on the train at seven thirty, on the job at eight thirty. And when his co-workers arrived at nine, his dexterous hands had calculated hundreds of numbers and were rattling on. Harvie Guthrie early again, making his co-workers look inefficient in manager Davidson's eyes. As they saw it, Harvie was challenging them to match the volume of work created by his dexterous hands. What was Harvie trying to prove?

So. He had his dexterity. They tried to interrupt his work with conversation. Seeing that they had to compete with the chatter of his machine, they gave up. Harvie was no conversationalist, they sighed. He was dull, no denying that, standoffish, in order that he might stand out, they explained, not having understood him.

Harvie Guthrie not understanding himself of late. It was during the last year on the job that Harvie felt something tugging at him, that he felt if he contemplated his having to go to work, he would not have gone. Or that if he did not leave home immediately, he would not have left at all. And that, once in the office, he had to engage his hands, so that he would not think of the static state of his life.

After work he would telephone Nellie, plead with her to come to him. She was reluctant to go to him when his voice sounded too urgent. She knowing that he used her, knowing that his flowing inside her was all that she would have of him, remembering his thrusting toward some undefined thing which had nothing to do with her. How she loved him. Nellie wanting to understand.

Harvie impatient. The bus crawling like a caterpillar through the street, its brakes sighing. Getting off, looking around him. Yellow-helmeted and ruddy-skinned construction workers sitting in a row outside an old building, eating donuts, drinking hot coffee. Greeting women with light absurdities, suggestive whispers, charming smiles from them, jostling each other. Their hands and clothing muddy, their eyebrows sand-fringed.

Harvie thinking how involved are they in their leisure. How involved are they in constructing the building rising opposite. Every man having a job to do, every man seemingly satisfied. The freest of men are those who choose their own work and who are satisfied. When they have completed the building, they will be able to point to it with pride because they built it.

But what can Harvie claim having built? Certainly, he has his dexterity.

Hesitating in the lobby of Chalmers Employment Agency. What if he has lost his dexterity? What if his hands have become

useless from idleness? What if he does not like the work he is as-
signed to? If he *gets* the job. It is not a question of liking. It never
was. He has to work, has worked all his life.

Still hesitating. He is not lazy; but his hesitation is indicative of
something. Harvie self-evaluating, self-critical. Do not seek to
disapprove. Seek to know. Objectivity is part of wisdom. There is
something of the vagrant in everyone. And given the opportunity,
most people would exchange their work for other work, or elect
to do nothing at all.

Harvie thinking of Nellie again. She on the job hard at work.
He dangling. Go on, Harvie Guthrie. Sinew and thrust.

Harvie handing his application to the woman behind the desk,
taking his seat again, watching her look over her nose at the application. He thinks her nose is situated unusually high on her
face, or so it seems. Looking away as she looks up.

"You didn't put anything beside 'Reason for leaving,' Mr.
Guthrie."

"I'd rather not. I meant to leave it blank." Embarrassed that
the other applicants sitting in the waiting room have heard her
accusing voice and are looking at him.

"Will you fill those in, please," in a forceful tone, pointing the
application at him.

Harvie writing "advance" beside "Reason for leaving." Taking
his seat again. Feeling a strange humiliation at sitting and waiting to be called for interview by someone who holds a power over
him as to whether he will eat or starve. If the interviewer is anything like the receptionist—

"Mr. Guthrie, you'll have to take a five-minute test on the adding machine. Calculate these numbers. Choose any one of those
machines."

Harvie feeling his hands growing warm.

"You may start." Setting the timer. "Time is up when the bell
rings."

Harvie's fingers growing hot, nimble. He has calculated the
numbers twice, his fingers calculating a third time. The bell.

The receptionist taking the paper from him into an inner office,
coming out again. "Mrs. Brown will see you, Mr. Guthrie."

"I've just finished looking over your test results, Mr. Guthrie," Mrs. Brown smiling. "You've calculated those numbers faster than anyone else we've had. We certainly want to hold on to you. Your dexterity. Where did you get such speed and skill?"

"It's more or less knowing how to read numbers and knowing how to operate the machine." Feeling arrogant. He has not lost his dexterity.

"What you're saying is that it takes practical experience. Well, you have it. When will you be ready for work?"

"Today." Feeling anxious. Does his interviewer notice his anxiety?

"We don't have a job for you today; but we should have something before the end of the week."

The end of the week. Harvie could be out of a place to stay, could have starved to death by the end of the week. "There's plenty of time, Mrs. Brown," feigning indifference. "You have my telephone number when you need me."

"I'll call you this week, Mr. Guthrie. Goodbye."

Harvie at the exit, feeling at loose ends again. What will he do with all of this time? He could spend it with Nellie. But she has to work today. Harvie longing for her.

He will engage himself, play the pinball machine in the Arcade. He is surprised by the number of employable men playing the pinball machines. The clock in the City Hall striking two. Harvie thinking about Hardy Gallant. Where is he now? What is he doing? He does not know why he is thinking of Hardy at this moment. Perhaps he connects him with the idle men playing the pinball machines.

But Hardy's idleness was due to circumstances, though he never said what the circumstances were. He merely said he lost his job over truth. And he kept saying to Harvie that he had to keep in touch, kept using the expression *keep in touch*, as if it were an oracle.

Harvie thinking of all the beers he drank with him, thinking about Hardy's insistence that the empty bottles remain on the bar. There must have been more than fourteen bottles, total. Of course, he hadn't forgotten their having sung and played the harmonica in the street. They counted fifteen dollars in their collection of coins given them by passers-by. Harvie thinking that the entertainment, more than their circumstances, attracted most of the people to them. Hardy Gallant had a sense of humor, charm, innovation. And Harvie could not accept him as a mere beggar. There was something about his nature that belied his beggarly occupation and psychology. But as Hardy told him, he, Harvie Guthrie, was no judge of people. Shrugging his shoulders.

Releasing a pinball, driving it hard. Bang. Thinking that by next Christmas Eve, Hardy Gallant will have drunk himself to death, frozen in an abandoned doorway, or he will have tried to bring the goodness out of the wrong person. And yet, he did not believe his thoughts.

Tilting the pinball machine. Steady. Not so good. But what does he expect? It isn't every day that he gets a chance to play the pinball machine at two o'clock in the afternoon. If he were still working, he'd have been back from lunch an hour now. Wondering who is using his machine. Well, Mr. Davidson would miss him. And Harvie has been faithful.

See how the faithful are rewarded? Realizing that he was just another tool for the job, the other part of the machine. Had the machine reacted to Harvie, Mr. Davidson would have decided the machine needed repairing. But then, Harvie reacted to the machine, and Mr. Davidson decided that Harvie needed replacing. Harvie being analytical. Too late.

Shooting another ball, does not care where it goes. Another thrust. Boom. The lights blinking. Enough. He has spent his quarter, used his hands. Now what shall he do?

The man playing the pinball machine next to his is intent upon the game, aggressive, demanding, concentrating upon the ball. Tilting the machine, pounding it with both palms. Score. He has feeling for the game. He knows what the machine does and what he can do. He is cool, relaxed in his playing.

"You play the game often?" Harvie.

"Yeah." Boom. Blink, blink, blink.

Harvie feeling that he is intruding, retreats, notices the woman walking back and forth before the open entrance to the Arcade looking at Harvie, hoping to attract his interest, walking away from the window while still looking at Harvie. Shall he follow her, answer her solicitation and thereby end his static feeling? Accord is what he needs. And he can find accord only with Nellie.

Sweet Nellie. His longing for her growing until he thinks he will explode. Passing the woman outside the Arcade without looking at her. The wind is wild, blowing everyone, upsetting vegetable and fruit baskets along Market Street, lifting dust and driving it into his eyes with a howling, insistent sweep. Move on, Harvie Guthrie. Move on.

Nellie switching on the transcription machine, fitting the earphones to her ear lobes, listening. Miss Watson's voice. Her letters are essentially of the same tone, of the same wording, so that without listening Nellie can almost type verbatim what Miss Watson will dictate. Nellie, having worked at J. P. Tomlin & Co. for five years, has not been absent one day of that time, excluding holidays. Shifting the typewriter carriage and typing the letter's close. Yours faithfully.

Nellie misses the large volume of letters and follow-up letters and reports which Miss Watson used to dictate. There used to be more work than she was able to finish in a day and always there was more coming from Miss Watson. Nellie feeling no longer useful since the volume declined. She feeling that her job is ceremonial, that she is secretary in name only.

Placing her foot on the pedal of the transcription machine, hearing Miss Watson's voice address her as if Miss Watson is there in the room. Nellie remembering her interview with Miss Watson . . . "I like you, Nellie. I think we'll get on well together. Are you married or engaged to be married?"

"Neither."

"Good. We don't have to worry about losing you for a while." Nellie wanted to tell her not to rely upon that, that she was hoping; she loving Harvie and waiting for the day when he would come to her with love as well as desire for her. Harvie is a quiet man, never talking about himself and Nellie. Restless man.

Nellie wondering what is Harvie doing. She will not telephone him, will never make him feel crowded, pushed. She will be to him as she has always been; she will be available, the loose tie that binds them, that links her greatest hope.

Other women waited for their men, took strength in being needed. Nellie having waited, having given what other women gave, feels that she should be no less than loved, Nellie loving. Nellie is human, too.

Adjusting the earphones, slowing Miss Watson's taped voice. A word she cannot understand. Nellie still remembering the time Miss Watson beckoned her to the chair beside her desk, and saying: *"Now tell me about yourself,"* looking first at Nellie's face and swiftly the length of her to her shoes, her eyes remaining there for a time. Nellie felt uneasy in the unusual quiet in the office. And she felt self-consciously that there was something inappropriate about the design in her stockings, that she should not wear them to the office. *"Why do you want to work here, Nellie?"* Miss Watson continuing her interview.

"I want to do work that is important and helps people. Work that means something more to me than just a paycheck."

"Oh?" Miss Watson leaning back in her chair.

"I want to like the work I do, relate to it because it needs human quality. Do you understand what I mean? Some work is so mechanical."

"Is that what you came here looking for?"

"You have to look somewhere. When you think you have to work all of your life, it isn't too much to ask that work mean something. That's how you measure your life, how you count the time spent, by the work you do."

"I'm surprised. I should think you'd be wanting to have fun. I envy your youth, Nellie." Staring, smiling. *"You're a brave young lady. You'll be a lot of help to me. As time goes by, you'll be getting more responsibility. If you have any concerns, if anything troubles you at any time, tell me about it. I wouldn't want to lose you because you're unhappy. Tomorrow is another day, Nellie. We'll start fresh in the morning. . . ."*

Correction. Pressing her foot down on the treadle, listening.

She does not have to erase. Every word she has typed up to this point is correct. Nellie pushing the carriage release, the letter keys, then period. Another routine letter.

Nellie feeling sedimental—just so much settled matter. Miss Watson is acting strangely toward Nellie, of late. Nellie feeling that she is deliberately denying her the opportunity to express her capabilities and treating her abruptly when she is in the office, dropping papers and pencils behind her desk and summoning Nellie to retrieve them.

Nellie walking into Miss Watson's office to look out of the window. Blue sky, white clouds, sun bright, the window washer lifting the scaffold left then right. The sky is full of shapes and colors, Nellie. The shape and color depend upon the time of day, the temper.

The clock on the City Hall striking five. Harvie waiting for Nellie at the exit of the building where she works. She will be pleased. He never before having had the time to meet her. Men and women of all sizes coming out of the building. Beautiful women and ugly women. Harvie Guthrie with time to watch the women. Thinking that watching women is the sole occupation of some men.

Nellie rushing down the steps of J. P. Tomlin & Co. with her career-woman bearing, determined toward home. He has never seen this Nellie before. She does not see him, and he cannot rely upon her coming in his direction by chance. Advance, Harvie Guthrie. Touching her lightly on the shoulder, startling her from her thoughts—who is this man?—recognizing him.

"Harvie, what are you doing here? Is something wrong?" Her mild eyes still asking the question.

"No. I thought I'd surprise you and wait. Does there have to be something *wrong?*"

"No. I'm surprised to see you here, that's all. You look out of sorts. Job hunting, I'll bet. Did you find anything?"

"Something temporary. They're going to call me."

"It's a start. It's what you wanted, a start. What have you been doing with the rest of your day?"

"Killing time. Waiting for you. Come home with me, Nellie."

Her mild eyes searching his, recognizing the old necessity. "All right, Harvie. I'll cook dinner for you."

Harvie knowing that he will not be able to sit watching her set the table, peel potatoes, wash and put them in the pot. He would not be able to sit watching her slice onions for his favorite onion rings. Harvie, feeling intensely static, just couldn't.

"No, Nellie. Let's eat out."

Nellie's lips framing a protest. She is concerned about his not being able to afford it.

"A celebration of my having found a job. Even though I don't have a real job, exactly."

She likes a celebration whenever she can celebrate, smiles. "All right," taking his arm.

"We'll eat at The Cafeteria, if we can get through all of these people. We'd better decide which direction we're going quickly, or they'll trample us running for the bus."

"They're anxious to get home, Harvie. That's natural."

"You don't run like that."

"But I'm always anxious to get home."

"Is Miss Watson still giving you trouble?"

"She's away. Didn't I tell you? It's not so bad when she's away. I want to hear about your job."

"I'll tell you about it after we eat," leading her into the cafeteria.

At The Cafeteria. She is still there bending among the tables, wiping away the crumbs, corrective shoes following, or leading. The uniform with apron made to fit, the curvature of her spine, the back of her cinnamon wig battened down with fine brown netting.

Harvie, looking at her. He doesn't know exactly why he finds her presence bothersome. Does she normally work long hours or is she working overtime today?

"Aren't you hungry, Harvie? You're not touching your food."

"Have you ever seen someone you pitied and hated at the same time, Nellie?" Cutting his steak and nodding toward the little woman edging among the tables.

"Why do you feel that way about her, Harvie?"

"I don't know. Maybe it's the way she does her work. It's agitating. She moves as if she hasn't any life in her—no, she moves as if nothing matters, as if she hasn't a care."

"Maybe she hasn't. It's still possible, even in this age."

"Maybe."

Harvie has finished his steak dinner almost as soon as he has begun. Now he must agonize over Nellie's slow, meticulous picking at her food. Food is for eating.

"You've finished *already*, Harvie."

"Hurry and eat and let's get out of here."

Nellie frowning at his impatience.

"I didn't mean it the way it sounded. I'm just restless."

"My big, voracious lion. Get some of that strawberry ice cream. You like strawberry. I'll be finished by that time. I won't have dessert."

"No. I'll smoke a cigarette." Breathing fire.

At his uptown place. Feeling joyously alive, snatching Nellie up in his arms. "Sweet lioness. Sweet Nellie."

CHAPTER

4

Harvie getting off the bus, the sound of his feet confirming his movement. Harvie Guthrie, worker-at-large, out of the mainstream. Harvie, temporary worker, approaching his new role.

Ahead, the flood of backs yielding ground to people behind. The onslaught of faces, moving forward, night's shade still about their eyelids. So significant the varying postures indicative of how the workers get on in life, are getting on.

Street cleaners pushing the dirt; door polishers putting on the shine; sewer cleaners digging deep. A young woman carrying a clock. A sleepy-eyed, puffy-eyed man running for the bus, the bus pulling away without him. Now he has time to tie the necktie stuffed in his pocket.

Harvie staring at the traffic light, hot and heavy hands thrust in his pockets. The traffic policeman blowing his whistle. Harvie has the go-ahead. Now that his opportunity to work is here, he does not rejoice, does not need what he has already got. Harvie Guthrie still complicated.

Leslie & Leslie. The elevator operator, a smiling little man with thinning white hair and hearing aid, tilting his head so that his hearing aid will better register the voices coming toward him.

The office workers call their floor numbers; but he knows the workers and he knows to what floor they are going, having taken them up every day, having brought them down. Turning to Harvie, looking him fully in the face, silently asking the question: where does Harvie want to go?

"Five, please."

"*Five?*" Wanting to understand; his hearing aid is not perfect. "*Five?*" Stopping at the fifth floor, nodding as Harvie gets off.

"Good morning. I'm Harvie Guthrie from Chalmers Agency."

"Yes, Mr. Guthrie; we've been expecting you. We're very informal here—you don't mind my calling you Harvie?—I'm Anne, the office manager." Anne Bowers, middle-aged, white hair interspersed with black, nodding to her left. "There's Sarah Himes, and Jim Taylor sits there. He's not in yet. You'll be working at this desk. Are you familiar with this machine?"

"Yes. I can use it." Harvie looking at the uncovered, dirty machine. Hardened food stains on the keys, between the keys. Coffee stains on the desk, dust and hardened chocolate stains. Loose paperclips and stained note paper. Tobacco grains.

"The man who works at this desk is in the hospital. He worked late evenings, so he ate as his desk—I'll clean it for you. Meanwhile you can sit there."

Harvie hesitating before the swivel armchair.

"Here, Harvie. I'll dust that for you. Dave was too busy to notice, I guess. And you couldn't expect him to. That's the cleaning woman's department. I think Dave worked too hard. He developed congestion in his chest. The doctors haven't said what it is. Poor Dave. They said he'd be in the hospital for a week. It's two weeks passed and he's still there. We talk to him over the phone. He says he doesn't know when he'll come out. He must be sicker than he thought." Anne sighing, dusting.

"You don't think it's t.b., do you, Anne?" Sarah coughing through cigarette smoke. "I mean, the reason why it's so secret. They ought to know what he's got by now. You think he knows and just isn't telling us because he's afraid he'll lose his job—or something?"

"Sarah! Dave doesn't have t.b. They would have told him by

now. Besides, he's feeling much better. He keeps asking if the
work is piling up. I told him that there's quite a bit of work; but
that his first concern is to get well. We don't want him to come
back too soon and have a relapse."

"Of course we don't, Anne. But he never looked like the strong-
est man I ever knew. You saw how he always took medicine."

"Oh. He took vitamin pills because he didn't always have time
to eat. You remember. He took vitamins with his bouillon. And
his black coffee. He drinks too much coffee. He drinks it all day.
He has so much work; he needs an assistant. You know how those
orders come in and how often the phone rings when Dave is here.
Sometimes he's talking to two people at a time and there's a man
or two waiting in the reception room to talk to him. The only
thing is, you didn't realize how much work he really did until he
got sick. The front office has to do a lot of his work now, except
the billing." Anne putting a final touch to the desk. "There you
are, Harvie. That's much cleaner than it was. You can change
things to suit yourself. Maybe you'll want to move the adding
machine. You arrange your desk to please yourself. You'll be
doing the billing."

Harvie nodding at the pile of papers date-stamped a week ago,
two weeks ago. Powerful Soap Chips—sixty-second commerical
to be used on the *Let's Stop This Nonsense Show*. Fine Boxed
Coffee, sixty-second commercial to be used on the *Joan Louise
Show*. Fine Bottled Coffee, one-page advertisement for *The
Weekly Reader*. Harvie trying to settle himself in the gray swivel
chair worn around the edges. Thinking that the gray office desks,
chairs, typewriters, the drab green walls within and the view of
the back stairs of an adjacent office building compound the static
within him.

"Good morning, ladies and gents."

"Good morning, Jim." Anne. "There's Harvie Guthrie."

"Hi, Harvie," Jim, medium height, balding, nearsighted behind
the thickness of his glasses. His shirt collar worn. Tossing two
mystery detective novels on his desk, along with a bag of lunch.
"Is he going to do Dave's work, Anne?"

"Harvie's going to do only the billing."

"Oh. What agency are you from?"

"Chalmers."

"Oh. Yes. Remember the woman we got from Chalmers? What was her name, Anne? Minnie, I think—wasn't it? Remember she couldn't do the work?"

"I remember her, Jim. You remember her, too, don't you, Sarah?"

"Of course I do, Anne. She was that typist we had. She made so many typing mistakes."

"And she said we were all against her. She said we changed what she typed to make it look like she made the mistakes. She was funny, wasn't she?"

"She was, Anne. Those people from the agency—it's hard to get someone who's good. Don't you think so? They're always walking away from the job." Jim picking up his coat from the chair. "I'll be back. Forgot to hang up my coat." Rushing back almost as soon as he left. "Anne. Somebody has taken my hanger again. This time I had my name on it."

"I know, Jim. The best way to prevent someone taking your hanger is to get in ahead of them, I guess."

"Put your hanger in you desk drawer at night." Sarah. "That's what Anne and I do."

"I'll *have* to. I put my coat on a hanger with someone else."

"Everybody ought to have their own hanger." Anne Bowers, polishing her glasses.

"They ought to buy enough hangers for the extra people, even if they are only *temporary*," Jim Taylor looking at Harvie through his bifocals. But Harvie does not respond, is not there, his not being there being important, if he is to remain there. How his hands fly over the keys, adding charges for commercial time. Ellen Yvonne's Soap Chips, ten-second commercial, December billing. Dexterous fingers spanning the keys, nimble fingers, communicative. Contact. Jim looking from Harvie to Anne. "Do you know, we throw away hangers at home. Mother used to save them."

"How's your mother, Jim?"

"She's fine except for her arthritis; and it bothers her mostly in bad weather," clearing his adding machine, spitting on the tip of his thumb with which he separates a volume of papers, pushing the total key on his adding machine again and looking at Harvie. "I hope the noise from my machine doesn't bother you, Harvie."

"It won't bother me." Harvie able to calculate and converse at the same time.

"How long have you been with Chalmers, Harvie?"

"This is my first assignment with them," fingers moving masterfully, swiftly. Sub-total.

"Oh." Jim clearing his machine for the third time. Rumble.

"Harvie's an efficient worker, Jim. He doesn't talk much," Sarah Himes tapping a cigarette on the edge of the desk, putting it between her lips, lighting it. "Remember that little Jeannie that was so quiet? She didn't work like Harvie, though."

Harvie smiling, lighting a cigarette, hands again in touch with the machine, adding dollars per second, minute. Soon it will be lunch time. The clock on the City Hall striking eleven.

5

Harvie will walk on his lunch hour. He cannot sit, not even for the length of a sandwich. Wanting to think. A walk to the waterfront will provide him with a free atmosphere for thinking. His nimble hands in his pockets, cigarette between his lips. Fire and smoke. Huff and puff and blow. Harvie leaving behind him the clatter of office machines, passing warehouses and factories, sniffing the aroma of chocolate rising from the candy factory. Tossing the cigarette, taking his harmonica from his pocket, blowing hard, a long wailing note, followed by another. A breath of feeling in one repetitive note.

A street vendor turning chestnuts over a fire. "Get them hot."

A one-legged beggar clutching a handful of pencils. "I am a veteran of the wars," reads the sign on the cigar box containing other pencils. His stump of a leg tucked inside his trousers, dangling.

Harvie breathing a wailing, rippling note into his harmonica. His long body swaggering. The odor of stagnant water, the chill of wind coming from the waterfront. Free air that makes its own direction, never looking back.

Ships anchored at the dock, husky men unloading cargo. Beyond the ships the open sky. An airplane gliding in the glare of the noon sun, reflecting silver light. White clouds gliding over the water. Sea gulls hovering, dipping. The wind rough, tugging at Harvie firmly bracing against the wind. Lighting another cigarette, watching the white smoke from the factory stretch skyward, blend with the clouds.

Harvie's thoughts fluent upon the water, flowing out. What is the feeling inside him wanting expression, wanting satisfaction? Looking over the stagnant water, himself feeling stagnant. Only his hands are alive, do not suffer from immobility, he depending upon his hands.

Nellie makes him feel alive, mobile. With Nellie his whole self feels necessary. She sets him in motion. But he and she are lunch hours apart; better that his body remain dead, lest he be unable to contain himself.

Blowing warm breath into his hands, rubbing them together like two pieces of kindling, hands which, though cold in the winter air, will with constant stimulation become afire. Then, can Harvie Guthrie say that only when bodies meet can there be any real movement, any real meaning? Sliding the harmonica across his lips, once, twice. A medley of notes without melody.

Looking at his watch. Time to return to the office. Harvie pounding the ground back to the office, hands in his pockets hot against his thighs. The aroma of chocolate flowing across his nostrils. The icy wind animating his footsteps. Move on. Exact in movement, the wind knows its man.

The bells tolling in the cathedral where the body of the dead worker lies, the late leader of the lowly employed, the underpaid, the unemployed. The late leader of the workers. *Work for the night is coming when man's work is done,* the church bells ringing a medley of hymns. Good men are missed. Bad men make room. All rest without labor.

Leslie & Leslie. The partially deaf elevator operator waiting on the ground floor. Harvie is ten minutes early, has time to kick his stall before entering it.

"Five?" the elevator operator.

"Yes. Five."

"Five." The old man lifting the elevator with a turn of the wheel, the hearing aid protruding from his ear, his eyes concentrated on the door. The elevator ascending, slowing, descending a little, stopping. "Five, sir," speaking in his thin voice, smiling, bowing.

Harvie stepping from one boxcar into another—the office. The machines will be quiet for a little less than ten minutes, when the lunch hour will end.

Ferne Darling, typist working in the outer office, pressing the shift key, typing *R* followed by *u n a m u c k*, laughing to herself. Runamuck. Ernest *G r i n d e*. What an appropriate name for a worker. Ferne playing games with work, chasing the humdrum of typing address labels and envelopes. Thinking: Ernest lives in Runamuck and his life's a Grinde. There's a good one. Thinking that if she can continue the game for another day, she will have gotten through another week with her mind intact. Weep for the people who work year-round with only two weeks vacation in the summer.

Ferne Darling's work ends at the first sign of spring. Spring is for blooming. Ferne, being a nature child, blooms in the spring, sunning, funning. She has her compensation.

Shifting the carriage. *L o v e*'s Park, Illinois. *B r o th w e l l*. *F r o i d*, Montana. *T h i e f* River Falls, Montana. John *D o o l i t - t l e* — Ferne Darling's philosophy: Do as little work as possible.

Stretching her arms, her fingers spreading like tarantulas, yawning. Quickly closing her mouth, upon seeing Harvie. "Harvie. I heard you saying your name this morning. I'm Ferne Darling. I'm from an agency, too. How do you like that den you're working in? Don't you feel caught?"

"No. I'm too busy."

"You're being a gentleman. I'm out here but I hear some of the conversations they keep in there. Weird."

"How long have you been here?"

"One long month. How long have you been working with your agency?" Embracing her typewriter, resting her chin on top of it. She has a slight dimple in her chin.

"This is my first assignment. I needed to work right away, so I took this until I find a permanent job. What about you?"

"I'm not looking for anything permanent, Harvie. This lifeless routine isn't for me. It's nothing but a rut. I saw a woman go berserk in an office. She just got up and started walking around the office, sat down; then she got up again and went over to the office manager's desk and started screaming at her. Don't laugh. They had to take the woman out. That's security for you, Harvie. Hospitalization and fringe benefits, then your mind explodes trying to cope, and you can't work any more. Or you can remain calm and work your way to a gold watch. It's frightening, Harvie. I prefer *my* way," flinging a hand at Harvie.

"The way you express your feelings about work—you know, I'd like to talk to you sometime. Maybe we could have lunch. You feel something like I feel. A whole eternity is going by and here I am pushing keys on an adding machine. And it doesn't really matter—not to me, not to these poeple. If I don't do it, somebody else will. I don't have to ask myself if I can do the work; it's a pushover. I'm tangled in life; but I don't feel my part in it.

"Look at the life of the leader of the workers whom they're going to bury tomorrow. He knew his part in life and he took it. He lifted people up and gave them hope. He even went beyond hope and gave their hope tangibility because they could see a change in their life because of him. He made them feel human. He showed them dignity, identity.

"He made you see the inequities of life and you wanted to kill everything that wasn't humane, that wasn't excellent. He was a man. He influenced life. He's my idea of a man who reached the summit of his capacity before he died. He had done as much as he could do and there was nothing left for him to do. So he didn't die in vain. No man succeeds himself. He lets go or he's pried loose. That's what death is. The people he helped—the migrant workers, porters, street cleaners—they've lost their leader, but he left them a path to better life. Do you know what I mean?

"I envy them their struggle. If mine were similar, I'd understand my discontent. But I get a good salary. I just haven't suffered."

"I know how you feel. I used to feel the same. I joined his marches and yelled slogans; but I really didn't feel that I was a part of what I was marching for. I wasn't involved even though I was there. Then one day I discovered what the trouble was. I had no commitment."

"Commitment. I never thought of it that way."

"Well, you know what I did about *that?*"

"What?"

"I decided that I would get married."

"*You?* You don't seem like the domestic type."

"I'll do my best. Why aren't you planning a wedding? Surely it's not a lack of eligible ladies—or are you the kind of man who loves himself, excluding all others?"

"I didn't say that I'm not married. But I'm not. My life is too much of a whirlpool right now. I don't understand myself half the time."

"Go on."

"It's the way I told you. I don't feel real, solid. I don't feel I belong. I spend most of my time being introspective and moody, and I keep telling myself I need more time. But I have time. I have all the days and nights; but I spend them doing things like sleeping. I tell myself that I'm acting ungrateful—that there are men who would gladly do the job I'm doing if they were trained. And then again I say that it has nothing to do with being ungrateful. It has nothing to do with self-love. It has nothing to do with my wanting too much. All I want is to do something important with my life. I want to sit down and read and think about life. I want to learn about life, about the worthwhile things, to prepare myself for what I really want to do. And I don't know what that is. My life is worth nothing as I'm living it now."

"The difference in us is that while you brood about the way your life is going, I rely on games to help me through mine. I'd lose my mind if I didn't."

"Listen, Ferne, I walk down to the waterfront on my lunch hour."

"That's dangerous," Ferne dipping her chin into her cupped hands.

"Maybe you'd like to walk with me tomorrow, maybe."

"Should I take a blanket to spread on the grass, so that we can sit and watch the icy water in twenty-degree weather? And if we're lucky, we'll have a nice strong wind. Harvie, do you want me to catch my death? It's not spring, you know. I can think of better ways to get away from it all."

"It was just an idea. I thought you'd like to walk. The air feels good after you've been inside all day. And we could talk."

"We've been talking."

"What's five or ten minutes? We wouldn't have talked *that* long, if I hadn't come from lunch early. I need somebody like you to talk to. I'm all bottled up inside."

"Why do you think you can talk to *me?*"

"You could give me insight."

"There you are—thinking about yourself."

"Is it wrong for one to think about oneself, to try to understand oneself? What harm would it do if we talked?"

"All right. I'll have to double my yogurt to protect me against the weather."

"Then you're going?"

"I'm going."

"I'll make certain it's not too cold," Harvie waving, going into the inner office.

The adding machine waiting, cold on the desk. Harvie sitting down, preparing to engage his hands, dexterous even in tedium.

"Harvie, how do you like it so far?" Anne blowing on her glasses, wiping them. "Are you interested in coming to work for us permanently?"

"No, thanks. I'm not ready for a permanent job yet."

"Oh. It's like that, is it? I hope you'll stay until Dave comes back?"

"I'll try," Harvie smiling.

"You'll be helping us quite a bit. Dave seems to be pretty sick."

"I hope he gets well soon. The hospital should heal him fast."

"I hope so," Anne busying herself with papers on her desk.

Ferne Darling typing and amusing herself. *N o r m a l*, Illinois. *C i r c l e v i l l e*, Ohio. *B l y t h e v i l l e*, Arkansas. *D e f i - a n c e*, Ohio. Then, letting her thoughts drift: She is standing before a judge. The place is Defiance, Ohio: *"Ferne Darling, you are sentenced to clerk typist."* Ferne replying: *"I defy you to try to make it binding,"* emerging from her fantasy smiling. Typing another envelope. Mr. Henry *M c M i l l i o n .* Henry make-a-million. What would Ferne Darling do with a million dollars? She would probably die of an overdose of money. Locking her hands behind her neck, yawning, looking around the office.

Mr. Lewis, the executive in charge, is talking on the telephone inside his glass-enclosed office. "I can't hear you, Bernice. This is a lousy connection." Calling to Florence, his secretary for twenty-five years. "Florence, will you call the operator?"

The president presented Florence with a diamond ring at a luncheon in the Green Room honoring her for twenty-five years service. Her picture is in the *Office News.* Middle-aged, well-preserved, beaming. She is working with the payroll and consulting Mr. Ames' assistant.

Every day for eight years, Mr. Ames has pulled his attendance card from the box at the receptionist's desk. Office assistants, as well as secretaries and clericals, pull their cards from the same box, placing them on the desk beside the box, indicating that they are present.

Ferne turning her attention to Nancy and Louise sitting at adjacent desks. As usual, Nancy is complaining.

"Louise, do you know that swelling in my knees hasn't gone away?"

"Why don't you go to the doctor, Nancy?"

"I will, Louise. I will. I'll go this weekend. You know, Louise, it's hard going to the doctor when you have to work every day. A lot of them don't have office hours on Saturday. Do you think it's my kidneys? I mean, that's rather serious—kidneys, I mean."

"I don't know, Nancy. Why don't you go to the doctor."

"You're right, Louise. The doctor will know," Nancy fidgeting with the papers on her desk, looking at Louise. "They'd probably want to do tests. Do you think so, Louise?"

"I guess it would depend, Nancy," Louise striking a typewriter key with an insistence.

"You're right, Louise. It would depend. If the swelling doesn't go down, I'll do what you said. I'll go to the doctor," shuffling the papers, lighting a cigarette. "You don't smoke, do you, Louise?"

"I used to, Nancy, but I stopped."

"That's what I should do—stop. Maybe that's part of my trouble, Louise?"

"I don't think smoking would have anything to do with swelling your knees."

"I didn't mean *that* so much. I meant generally."

"Well, Nancy, maybe if you got down to good hard work, you'd forget about it."

"You're right, Louise. If I didn't have anything to do, I'd go crazy thinking about myself."

Ferne typing again. *H u m a n s v i l l e ,* Missouri. *R u s h o-m o r e* Laboratory, *P a r a d i s e ,* Pennsylvania. Bartholomew *D e L o n g .* Ferne Darling thinking: De long day, smiling. Tiring of the game, going into the ladies' lounge to freshen her face.

"Anne, I got my coat hanger back," Jim rushing into the office. "I figured I'd get it back at lunch time. I'm going to keep it this time. I'll keep it in my drawer at night."

"That's right, Jim."

"Was Marie from Personnel here yet?"

"She looked in this morning."

"Did she say anything about Dave—when's he coming back?"

"No. I think she's ducking the issue. She's afraid we'll ask for more help. We need it, Jim. I don't see how Dave did all the work he did. I knew he was busy, but I never realized how busy. You know he reported to the front office, Jim. And I think they're planning to give us more work to do. That's why Marie sticks her head in the door and rushes off. She's afraid we have complaints. Sarah's still working on last week's commercials. And they're supposed to be rush."

"That's right, Anne. I feel tired, too. I have to go right to bed when I get home. You know how much I like to go out. I have to refuse most of my invitations during the week. My husband and I used to go out several times during the week when he was alive. Thank heavens we have Harvie to help us with the work."

Harvie's dexterous hands dancing over the keys, seeming to say: Let's get on with it. Soon it will be time to go home. The clock on the City Hall striking four.

CHAPTER

6

"Five?" The elevator operator adjusting his hearing aid, his thinning white hair soft as angel hair nodding at Harvie, smiling, sliding shut the elevator door. Harvie is five minutes late today. "We had a little snow," the elevator man turning his hearing aid toward Harvie. "Had a little *snow?*" tilting his head, waiting to pick up the reply.

"Yes, we did."

"Five." The doors gliding open, the old man nodding his angel hair. "Have a good day, sir."

"Good morning, Harvie. I see you managed to get back another day," Ferne Darling smiling. "But you had reservations, didn't you. Tell the truth," throwing a hand at Harvie. "For five minutes you stood in your apartment arguing as to whether or not you were coming to work."

Harvie laughing, looking for a hanger for his coat.

"Put your coat on top of mine. The red one with the fur collar."

"Thanks," carefully hanging his coat. "I don't want to wrinkle it."

"You can't harm it. It's been shot once. Rabbit's fur."

Harvie laughing louder than he should. His day is beginning

40

with a laugh. Waving goodbye to Ferne. "Don't forget lunch today," waving again.

"Good morning, Harvie," Anne Bowers walking into the office
with a cup of coffee. "Coffee cart's outside, Harvie. I can't do any
work until I have my coffee. It's not the best coffee, but it's coffee.
I have to have a cup to open my eyes when I get out of bed in the
morning; and I have to have one before I start work." Sitting
down, placing the coffee on a napkin.

"Good morning, Anne. The coffee's early today. I can use a
cup, too," Sarah lighting a cigarette. "Did Marie from Personnel
come by yet? I can't continue much longer, unless I get shorter
hours. I can't get over this cold. When I stayed home those two
weeks, it seemed to get better. I didn't have to get up so early."

"What did Marie say when you asked her about working half
days, Sarah?"

"She said she would see. But that was two weeks ago. Didn't
she say any more about it?"

"No. When she comes by, I'll ask her."

"I don't want to seem as if I'm pushing her. But don't you think
two weeks is enough time to wait for an answer? Anne, I'm sure
she won't say anything to me about it, *if* I don't say anything
more. She's hoping I won't ask, so she won't have to decide. Even
then she might say Leslie & Leslie can't use me any more, that
they're going to hire somebody else. It would be in their favor.
They would hire a younger girl, pay her less, and they'd have her
working full time. But I'll have to take that chance; my health's at
stake."

"I know, Sarah. Your cough doesn't sound as good as it did
when you first came back. I'd ask her."

"I'm going to. Isn't Jim here yet?"

"He called to say he had to take his mother to the doctor."

"Is she getting worse? Did he sound worried?"

"No. He said she wasn't feeling well and that he was going to
take her to the doctor. He'll be here later."

"What is it—her arthritis? She has arthritis, you know, Anne."

"I don't know, he didn't say. He said he was waiting for a cab
to take them to the doctor."

"Is his mother very old?"

"Well, Jim's about thirty-nine himself."

"He's forty. He told us once. You remember—when he first came to work."

"Yes, Sarah. I do remember. I wasn't far from remembering his age."

"No, you weren't. Where did Jim work before he came here? Wasn't he a typist somewhere? Wasn't that what he told us, Anne?"

"Yes. He was a correspondent."

"He's moved around quite a bit. I mean, he seems to have had quite a few jobs, Anne. He worked several places in Summerville. Then there was Doylestown. What do you suppose he's been doing with his life? Men Jim's age are executives, presidents and vice-presidents—in charge of something. He's not even an assistant manager. He's only a clerical worker. And he's not getting much more money than he got before he came here. He would have been getting less; but he told Marie he thought he ought to be getting more because he's a man. You remember he told us that, Anne. Then they use him at the secretary's desk when she's out. I suppose it ought to be worth something extra. They say he's a fast typist."

"I don't know, Sarah. Maybe he doesn't think of what he's doing the way you do."

"You think *not*, Anne? You notice how restless he gets? He'd rather not do what he's doing. He'd rather be out of this office than in. He likes going upstairs and relieving the secretaries. I think it's the responsibility; he has more responsibility. He can answer the phones, take shorthand, and he's a fast typist, and he uses the adding machine. He gets a lot of work done."

"I know he's fast; but he makes a lot of mistakes. You saw the memos he typed."

"I'm sure he does better upstairs, Anne."

"I hope so. Besides, those men in the executive offices won't let a letter go out if it isn't just right."

"I think there's Jim now."

"Good morning, ladies and gents."

"Good morning, Jim. How's your mother?"

"The doctor said she's doing well. She went for a checkup. Mother doesn't go out alone. Somebody has to be with her." Jim taking the coat hanger from his desk drawer. "Good morning, Harvie. I see you're still with us." Searching his coat pockets, emptying them of loose change. "Anne, do you know that it cost five dollars to ride a cab to and from the doctor? I'm going to have to ask for a raise. You know, they made five deductions from my paycheck last week. They deducted fifteen dollars for hospital insurance. You can imagine how much I had left. They weren't supposed to take it out all at once."

"Did you tell them, Jim?"

"Yes. I told them."

"Sometimes you have to remind them."

"I'm going to," slipping his coat onto the hanger. "You notice I have a coat hanger today. I was smart, wasn't I, Sarah— especially since I had to come in late. Did you notice that there are two coats on a hanger out there? I'm going to ask Marie for hangers, Anne. There ought to be more hangers. They can't pay a decent salary, so they ought to be able to buy enough hangers. When people like Harvie come to work, they can't get a hanger. I hope you don't think I'm going above your authority, Anne. You're in charge; but we need hangers. If I see Marie before you see her, I'll ask for you."

"Certainly, Jim."

"Harvie, if you're going to be coming in for a while, maybe you'd better grab a hanger and put it in your drawer. You'll be sure to have one."

"I don't care. I can always put it on my chair. Better still, I have a hanger mate. I'm sharing a hanger," Harvie's fingers commanding the keys, the tape hanging over the desk, onto the floor.

"Oh," Jim flushing, casting an insinuating glance at Anne, Sarah, going out to hang his coat, back again, sitting down, lighting a cigarette, watching Harvie between the streamers of smoke.

"Is that your coat on top of the one with the fur collar, Harvie?"

"Yes, the brown coat is mine," his dexterous hands recording numbers.

Jim looking at Anne, Sarah. "Is that the coat of the girl from the agency, Anne? What's her name?"

Harvie commanding the keys. Sub-total. Check.

"Yes," Jim. "The strange girl with the braided hair."

"She likes to stay in the office and eat yogurt and celery."

"Don't forget the carrot and beet juice, Anne; and the sun-flower seeds."

"Why does she eat it? It doesn't sound appetizing. Does she say, Sarah?"

"I heard she said that juices were easier to digest than the bulk —whatever that means," Jim waiting, watching for Harvie's reaction. Harvie is away, is with his dexterity, going, going.

"She doesn't eat meat. She says eating meat is like eating your next-door neighbor."

"She's got rabbit's fur on her collar. If she thinks so much of animals, why would she be wearing one around her neck?"

"Well, Jim, maybe she thinks it's only the rabbit's fur and not the rabbit."

"You would say that, Anne. I saw her eat fish once."

"Everybody eats fish."

"She reads strange books."

"What strange books?" Sarah.

"*Strange* books. I didn't memorize the names of the books."

"She has such a pretty face. You can't deny that her complexion is healthy. Her skin is a natural pink. When I was her age, I would have given anything to have a complexion like hers. I could use it now—especially now that I'm so old."

"You—*old*, Sarah? The way you get around to all those dinner parties?"

"I haven't done much getting around to dinner parties lately, Anne. I meant to ask, Jim, how's your girl friend? Is she any better?"

"No, Sarah. Half her intestines will have to come out soon."

"Oh, Jim! What a shame."

"She's not a bit sad, though. She's a brave, strong person. Anne, do you know, she's just as cheerful. What can she do about it? She says the important thing is that she get well. And she'll be well after the surgeons take out those bad intestines."

"You were supposed to get married, weren't you?" Sarah.

"Yes. But we'll have to put off the wedding for a few months. She said she doesn't want to get married until she's fully recovered from the operation. She's a nice woman and strong-spirited. Do you know that she goes to work every day and works a full day. I tell you, Sarah, I don't know how she does it. She must suffer something terrible—with the pain. But she has pills the doctor gave her. I'm paying all her doctor and hospital bills. I wanted us to marry so that I can take care of her. But she won't let us get married. She said it wouldn't be fair."

"When were you supposed to get married?"

"Next month."

"I'm very, very sorry to hear the bad news, Jim."

"That's the way it is sometimes, Sarah," Jim uncovering his adding machine, clearing the tape. "I guess the coffee cart has gone, huh, Anne?"

"Yes, Jim. It was here when I came to work this morning."

"You should have saved a cup for me."

"I thought you'd bring a cup when you came, since you were coming in late. Besides, it would have been cold by the time you came."

"You're right," Jim clearing his adding machine again, several times, furtively looking at Harvie. Ought, ought, zero, zero.

Harvie Guthrie is adding, sub-total, total; thinking of Nellie, feeling dead in every part of his body but his fingers. His life is in his fingers, in his hands, while his body begs to come to life, while the humdrum hours seep through his brain. The clock on the City Hall striking eleven.

He must not think. He must close his mind, lose himself in his dexterity. One question, though. Every man is allowed one question. There are shoeshine men who would feel like executives had they the ability to work with an adding machine. There are janitors, elevator operators, street cleaners, men in innumerable lowly jobs who wish they could do the job Harvie is doing, would be grateful for the chance. Harvie Guthrie intelligent and dexterous, working at a respectable job, free of the indignities of lowly employment, dissatisfied with what he is doing. Is Harvie going mad?

Dexterity is not enough. His hands were made to do more than punch numbers on an adding machine. Harvie has large, strong hands. There are joints in his fingers. When he wants his fingers to bend, they bend. When he wants to make a fist, he makes a fist; surely he has even more control over what his hands shall do.

When he was a child he made castles in the sand, launched ships, flew airplanes. But Harvie never lived in those castles, never sailed in his ships; and though he flew airplanes, he never left the ground. Harvie Guthrie, boy at play, is now Harvie Guthrie, man at work.

These hands were made to shape things, to round out the future; yet here he sits pressing numbered keys that leave their mark on tape that the machine spits out, that trickles down the side of the desk and is eventually thrown into the wastebasket, which is emptied by the cleaning woman at the end of the day.

Vital Harvie Guthrie, anesthetized—except when loving Nellie. He needing her now, wanting her. She makes him forget his frustration. Nellie, self-sufficient. One day Harvie will simply walk away from the job, go to Nellie's job and rescue her. Pushing the add key—once, twice, three times. Total. Looking at the gray wall outside. The clock on the cathedral tolling twelve.

Jim looking. "Anne, do you hear the bells tolling. It's for the dead leader of the workers."

"Yes. I hear them."

"What do you think, Anne?"

"I think it's sad."

"Yeah, I guess it is. How much do you think the funeral will cost? Do you know, Anne?"

"Oh, I don't know, Jim. He'll have a good funeral, of course, having been the man he was."

Harvie rising from his chair, pushing it against the wall. Great questions and issues are being raised and fought for. Great men are dying. And all that these people can discuss is the funeral cost. Walking from the office, lighting a cigarette.

"What did I say?"

"He's probably upset, Jim."

"But he's not—"

"I know; but he has friends, probably."

"Where do you think he went? Do you think he went home?"

"No doubt he went to lunch."

"Down? Down?" The elevator operator smiling for Ferne Darling and Harvie, nodding, the wire attached to his hearing aid half concealed beneath his white jacket, closing the elevator door, turning the wheel that lets the elevator down. "The weather's a little warmer. The snow's gone."

"Yes, it has," Ferne nudging Harvie, Harvie responding.

"Yes, it has gone."

"Have a nice lunch."

"Isn't he a sweet little man, Harvie? Did you hear his hearing aid making that noise?"

"No."

"What's the matter with you?"

"Let's walk."

"Do you know that he says the same thing every day. It's almost like he isn't real. You've heard those voices in the modern, self-operating elevators?"

"I know what you mean."

"You know the elevators with the recorded voice that say good morning and call the floors and you find yourself looking around the elevator for the voice. He reminds me of that. How far is the waterfront, Harvie?"

"I thought you were adventurous," Harvie smiling. "Does it matter how far?"

"Oh, I am. I *am*."

"Maybe I can find out why you're marrying a man you don't love."

"I'm preparing for my old age."

"You're preparing to trap yourself."

"And you're concerned, although I don't understand why. I'm not marrying *you*," flinging a hand.

"It's just that you were made to be free, loose. You're a bird of paradise. Trap yourself in a house with a clinging husband, clinging children, dirty dishes, clothes, marketing, entertaining your husband's associates—and you'll be running out into the streets raving. It'll be your own fault."

"Listen, Harvie. I've learned all I will ever know about love; and I know all there is to know about loneliness. I believe that it's better to live with someone you don't love than to live your whole life alone. I'm not a radiant beauty and I'm glad. I know that Frederick will take me for myself and when I'm old he will not grow tired of me because I've lost my beauty.

"Beautiful women have short lives. Even while they are beautiful they live in fear of the day when the first wrinkle will come, when their breasts will collapse and they have lost their only attraction. I don't have those fears. The only fear I have is of becoming an old, vagrant, lonely typist, an old nature child; but that's not a fear any more. I've solved that. I'll marry and keep my freedom, too. I'll not have any children."

"Did you tell him that?"

"Why should I tell him? If he doesn't mention it, why should I? Children take too much of life. I need all of my life to live. Why spend all of your life bringing up children who turn out to be monsters after all?"

"Are you a monster?"

"I haven't a *bit* of monster blood, Harvie Guthrie. Have you invited me for a walk so that you can insult me?" Ferne laughing.

"Then you won't have monster children," Harvie striding, hands swelling in his pockets, listening to Ferne's voice flowing through the chocolate-scented air. The sun is a yellow ball overhead. Laughter coming from a window of the chocolate factory. "I'll race you to the pier." Running, Ferne gamely running after him. Stopping, vapor running from their lips, at the land's edge.

"I'm out of breath."

"It's good exercise."

"Not for a girl who's had nothing to eat all day but yogurt," laughing.

"What happened to your sunflower seeds?" smirking.

"I think you're needling me. Are your little friends still talking about my diet food?"

Harvie laughing, striding to the fence put up by the workmen, thrusting his great fingers between the diamond shapes in the wiring, staring across the water. A dredging company, its thick-toothed crane dipping, biting the mud, spitting it out. Portions of the river marked off by thick wooden stakes sticking out of the water. The bridge stretching across the water to the left, to the right another bridge. Farther down the river a ship stands in the harbor. Sunbeams on the still water.

"You hold that fence as if you might go over, like a man who's been locked in too long," Ferne joining him at the fence. "What do you think they're digging for—dreams?"

"Could be. It's not an impossible place for finding dreams. But I have the feeling they're looking for something more tangible."

"Like rubbish," Ferne nudging Harvie, simultaneously giving him one of her mischievous glances, both laughing.

In the farther distance the high-rise office buildings flanking the City Hall, massive glass facades throwing off the sun's reflection. Great round clouds traveling en masse as if they gather forces for an onslaught upon some unseen alien in the sky.

"What's the good life, Ferne?"

"Well, with me, it's not having to work and living from what the land produces, picking flowers."

"But somebody has to plant or there'll be nothing for the land to produce."

"There are planters and there are reapers." Tossing her scarf around her neck, battening it down against the wind growing livelier, colder.

"I think the good life has something to do with a man's greatness."

"All right. You take greatness and I'll take treasure. I have never heard of a great woman, have you?"

"Women are different. They don't want greatness. They live for the greatness of their men."

"What if they have no great men. Do women who have no great men then die for want of a great man?"

"A great man feels greatness inside himself."

"So how does he communicate this greatness to the woman so that she can live his greatness?"

"If they are right for each other, they'll communicate."

"I prefer having something of my own—so much for greatness."

"But don't you think *he* was great?"

"He was great. But greatness is so distant; to me, greatness is not a man. I think it's more or less something that he generates beyond himself, that makes us think of him as something more than mortal. His wife saw him as her *husband*."

"But do you notice that with his dying the greatness that was so distant seems to have settled around us, continues."

"I think that's what's called the spirit."

"Yes. A great man." Looking at his watch. "We've got fifteen minutes to get back."

"We don't want to be late. It'll give them extra time to talk about us. What do you suppose they say when we're not there?"

"I'm not interested and I'm sure you're not interested either. We give them their significance by allowing them to take us apart verbally."

"Did you notice that, too? I think they don't like our independence. We work when we want to work and we still have work when we need it."

"I'm not competing with anyone. I've got my own pace to keep. What's wrong with us, Ferne?"

"There's nothing wrong with us that time off from work won't heal."

"I'm talking seriously."

"And you think *I'm* not serious?"

"What's wrong with our not wanting to be what we are employed to be?"

"What should we be?"

"I don't know! That's what's so scary. I don't know."

"Have you tried positive thinking?"

"Now you're needling me."

"Harvie, you're too complicated. Just *be*. All I want is free leisure, a plot of grass to lie on, and some sunflower seeds and *I am*. You can have everything if you don't want too much. I will have everything."

"Everything *materially*."

"Well, what *else*?"

"I am not certain that it is the material with me—it's too subtle."

"I like comfort, but I'm not greedy. Chasing shadows is not for me. Most of the time you end up finding out you've been chasing your own shadow; so where have you been, after all, except in a circle? No, Harvie, I'm going to lie in the grass in the sun and let the shadows pass by."

"A man needs more. It's simple for you because you're a woman."

"You're wrong. A woman *settles* for less." Staring at the traffic light.

"All right. Women settle for less." The traffic light changing. "We'd better be quick," passing The Oyster Bed restaurant, the slaughter houses, cargo trucks. A beggar sitting on the ground holding a box of pencils, exposing the bare nub of an amputated leg.

"Oh, it makes me sick," Ferne Darling turning away.

"That's what you call working on the public's conscience. I learned that from a friend of mine—a very funny fellow."

"Well, did the *public* maim him? It's like he's saying, 'See what *you* did?' "

"I think you're being too harsh. I'm sure he's not blaming anybody, but—"

"Do you know what I feel when I see people like him? Revulsion. That's what I feel. It makes me sick to my stomach."

"I thought there were organizations that helped people like him."

"There are. There was something in the paper the other day

about curbing that sort of thing—something about soliciting and
creating a public nuisance."

"I met a fellow at Christmas time. Hardy Gallant. I can't say he
was a beggar, even though he begged. That fellow had tre-
mendous insight into people and their reactions to beggars, and
he had a sense of humor; he was a very funny man, clever. He
kept saying, 'Bring the generosity out of the people.'"

"Was he a tall man with curly hair and boyish face?"

"Yes. Have you seen him?"

"I saw him in the park on the circle last summer. He was amusing. He sang songs. They weren't songs one would sing at a
ladies' tea. He was a pretty good ad-libber. What are you laughing about?"

"I sang Christmas carols with him."

"*You?*"

"Yes. *I* sang."

"Where?"

"In town."

"You were drunk, of course."

"Of course not. I wasn't myself, exactly; but I wasn't drunk."

"You don't seem like the type."

"It was Christmas and I felt like singing."

"You were drunk."

"I was not. I played the harmonica also."

"—and the ukelele—"

"You don't believe me. See." Holding up the harmonica.

"I'm convinced. Did I tell you about the woman who heard me
whistling in the woman's lounge? She asked if I was a professional whistler and if that was the reason for my working temporarily."

Ferne and Harvie laughing, mounting the steps to Leslie & Leslie.

"Five? Did you have a nice lunch?" the elevator operator smiling, bowing his head, listening to the hearing aid confirm that it is
a nice day and that Harvie and Ferne have had a nice lunch.

The clock on the City Hall striking one. The bells tolling in the
cathedral. The quiet procession bearing the workers' leader to

the cemetery. Maids, porters, office workers fathoms thick on the sidewalks, swollen eyes overflowing, looking after the procession. Goodbye, Champion.

Harvie thinking that while this man died after having achieved greatness, he will die in an office chair, dexterity and all. Or if he were luckier, he might die with Nellie. Spill over into her and die. Back to the womb. At least he did some kicking there. Some men were groomed to die magnificently.

"Anne," Jim walking into the office, pulling out his desk drawer to get his coat hanger, hanging up his coat. "You should have seen the procession," hesitating at the sight of Harvie. "It was so sad—the coffin and everything. All the people standing on the street looking. A man standing beside me cried out loud. It was so pitiful. I felt so sorry for him. Then he got down on his knees and prayed. You know, he had his rosary beads. And he was crying, 'My poor son.' He was the dead man's father."

"Father? If he was related he would have been at the funeral, Jim."

"Maybe he was late," Jim's face reddening. "The cars were driving away. You should have seen all of the people wiping their eyes. They're probably at the cemetery now."

"But the cemetery is beyond the city limits. It should take longer than that."

"You're right, Sarah. Any news from Dave, yet? When is he getting out of the hospital?"

"He says he doesn't know. The hospital doesn't know when they will release him."

"Oh," Jim looking alert. "He's taking a turn for the worse?"

"No. He's no worse, Jim. The doctors want to take more tests to make sure he's ready to go home. They wouldn't want to send him home too soon. And they can't tell how soon that will be until they've taken the tests and gotten the results."

"Oh. I'm glad it's not serious. Dave's a nice guy." Clearing the adding machine, looking at Harvie, at Anne. "Did he sound worried?"

"Not about himself. He was worried that the work was piling up. You know the office has called him several times to ask questions. He thinks they're having problems solving things because of him. I told him that we had Harvie helping us."

"He shouldn't feel that way. He couldn't help getting sick. There's no sense his blaming himself. He has to think of his health. Does he have a wife?"

"A wife and two children, Sarah."

"Is he doing something special—the reason why he has to work so hard?"

"I don't know, Sarah. He doesn't talk about his personal affairs. He mentioned his wife and children once, that's all I know."

"Well, I'm certainly not going to wind up in a hospital. I'm going to talk to Marie today. She'll probably ask me to resign."

"I don't think so, Sarah. She would probably rather you didn't go on part time, that's all. She thinks you'll get better while you're waiting for her decision and she won't have to do anything, I guess."

"I guess. I feel a little bad about asking her with Dave out sick and Harvie only temporary. But I have to look after my health."

"You do, Sarah."

"Excuse me, madam. I wonder if you would let me have the job section of the paper," Hardy Gallant, appealing to a startled woman looking up from her newspaper.

"This is an out-of-town newspaper."

"Sorry, madam. Terribly sorry," backing away, smiling.

"Didn't he have a nerve? What would he do with the job section?" Another woman standing nearby. "Why, he never worked a day in his life from the looks of him; and he's not the least bit interested in working now."

The woman smiling, looking again at the newspaper. They are burying the workers' leader today. Assembly-line workers are striking for more pay. Negroes appealing for equal job opportunities.

The clock on the City Hall striking five.

CHAPTER

7

"All right, Hardy. In exchange for keeping the heat going and sweeping the sidewalk, I'm going to let you live here rent-free. I'm going to take a chance with you. You're the superintendent of this building and you have a place to stay for as long as we keep the building open. As you can see, this is one of the few houses left on this street that is still occupied."

"Thank you, sir, for giving me this chance."

"As we relocate these people, we close the rooms—lock them—do you understand, so that no unauthorized person reoccupies them."

"Yes, sir. You can depend on me. I'll take care of everything."

"I'm counting on you, Hardy. If you have any questions, or any problems with the tenants, or if you decide to move on, I want you to let me know. This is a responsibility that you've taken on; and if you decide it's not the responsibility for you, you don't abandon it; you talk it over, let me know that you want to leave, and I'll get someone to replace you. Remember, there are people living in here who will be depending on you as the caretaker. They'll be depending on you to keep them supplied with heat and to keep the place clean and in operation. They'll be depending on you as my liaison man; you're the channel. Remember that, and you'll be all right."

"It's very kind of you, sir. You can count on me. If only there were more men like you who give men like me a chance. If I had a hat I'd take it off to you."

"Give me a little bit more of your background, Hardy. Your name is Hardy Gallant. What kind of work did you do when you worked? Have you been out on the streets long?"

"Not long, sir. But if it hadn't been for you—well, I would still be out there. It's hard sleeping in doorways, sir—especially hard this winter. If you know what I mean, sir. The wintertime is getting colder. Three of my friends froze to death within a month."

"I'm sorry, Hardy—"

"Are you, sir?"

"Well, certainly I'm sorry."

"Sir, I meant I could see how the news affected you—almost as if they were your own friends who froze to death."

"Well, I guess they had relatives who gave them decent burial."

"Yes, sir. I guess every man is related to something. It's whether or not he *wants* to be that matters."

"You're not wanted for anything, are you, Gallant?"

"*Wanted*, sir? No. I'm not wanted."

"I mean you're not in rogues' gallery—the police, anybody?"

"Nobody wants me, sir."

"That's good, Hardy. That's fine. That's what I like to hear. I recognize the right man when I see him. I've been dealing with men all my life, and I've never been wrong yet," slapping Hardy Gallant on the shoulder. "All right, Hardy, you take over. I'll be around to see how you're doing. Take this in case you need me."

"Don't worry, sir. I'll take care of everything," pocketing the card with the name Everett Bentley and telephone number, simultaneously waving off Mr. Bentley. Hands in pockets, looking at the house he will inhabit. A weather-beaten brownstone house. Hardy Gallant, out of the weather.

"Anchor the man!
Anchor the man!
He'll work himself to death.
Anchor the man!"

"Thank you for your concern, friends. If I had a hat I'd take it off to you." Hardy Gallant sitting back in a beach chair, part of the furniture in the large room in the brownstone house, formerly a townhouse, waiting for the evacuation of its tenants and finally demolition.

"Have you decided to desert us, Hardy, and become a citizen again?"

"That was a very nice song you composed for me, Stoney. Very nice. But, Stoney, remember one thing. We are the *dead*. A man can't work himself to death if he's already dead. But you've got to be a little realistic now and then. Keep in touch. Now, it's *cold* out there. Right, men?"

"Right."

"It was fourteen degrees yesterday, Hardy."

"Yeah. You heard about Sam and his brother. They were sleeping in that old newspaper shack and burned it down."

"Yeah. Poor Sam."

"What about his brother?"

"I didn't know his brother. But I'm sorry for him, too."

"What is it with the weather, though? It's even bad for the dogs."

"You know how Tony hates mission houses. He avoids them like they were his wife; but he stayed in one *last* night."

"You don't know nothing about me! And who says I have a wife?"

"Stop bristling up your feathers. I didn't say *you had* a wife. Listen to English. I was leading up to say you slept in the mission last night and that it had to be cold for you to do a thing like *that*."

"As I said, friends, you've got to be realistic. Keep in touch. Tony's realistic, so he stayed at the mission house. Well, Tony, no more mission house. You may bed at my house. You and the rest of my friends. I'm in charge of the fire. Fire means warmth."

"Anybody living here, Hardy?"

"Sure. Citizens live here. You've got to keep in touch, Tank. Now if there was nobody living in the house, wouldn't it be boarded like the rest that have nobody living in them?"

"I thought you staked it, Hardy."

"I thought you staked it, the same as Tank."

"You're out of touch, friends. How do you think I staked it?"

"I don't mean you *bought* it."

"Thank you; that goes without saying. What you mean is that I captured it with a hand grenade."

"I thought you moved in when no one was looking. That's what I thought."

"Well, in truth, I am being rehabilitated."

"Rehabilitated?"

"Is that why you wanted us to come here—so that you can talk about rehabilitation—you sold out? Is that what you did, Hardy, sold out?"

"Hardy wouldn't sell out. Would you, Hardy?"

"He did, didn't he? Right under our noses."

"Now he called us here to tell us how good it is to be rehabilitated."

"Hardy, we've bummed around a lot together, slept on the same floor; but I'll not let you rehabilitate me."

"No. We'll not hear any of that propaganda they told you to tell us."

"What did they do to you, Hardy? You were doing all right."

"He was making out better than some of us."

"That's because he's clever."

"Yeah. He's clever, all right. He let somebody rehabilitate him. *That's* how clever."

"Look. We're all a bunch of bums and we know it. We're not trying to be anything else. Hardy's a bum at heart, but he let them get to his head and fill it with ideas that he's not a bum."

"Yeah. That's what they did. They don't know him like we do. Remember how we found that old mattress and put it way back in the park last summer and five of us slept on it?"

"Yeah. Yeah. And remember how Tank woke up screaming? There was a pigeon walking on his head."

"Old Tank. We didn't know he could scream so loud."

"What would you do if something was on your head and you didn't know what it was?"

"At first we thought old Tank was drunk; then we saw the pigeon."

"And don't forget the time Tank made that whiskey or what-ever he called it that nearly killed us all—"

"And Tank was *really* near dead."

"Tank will drink anything."

"Well, what about *you?* I made it, but you drank some of it, too."

"Sure. I'll admit it. What's important is the results."

"Hardy here, he didn't drink so much."

"What did he say, Tank? You tell us how he said it."

"Yeah, Tank. You can imitate him better. How did he say it?"

"Well, he screwed up his face like this—"

"Do it, Tank. That's it."

"Ha. Ha."

"He screwed up his face like this and he said, 'Well, I'd better not take too much. If there's anything worse than having *not,* it's *excess.* So I'm going to moderate. I believe this stuff can put you away. And as you know, friends, I've got to keep in touch.'"

"Ha. Ha."

"Yeah, that's him. That's him—that's Hardy."

"And all the while he's screwing his face like this."

"That's him. That's him."

"Then he stretches his eyes and he says, 'That didn't go down. It evaporated!'"

"Wasn't that a night? Old blue eyes here was incoherent."

"Have you ever known him when he *wasn't?*"

"*All* of us went to the hospital."

"Those nice, warm, white sheets. I was embarrassed. It took me a while to get adjusted."

"And three meals a day."

"What did they call those little custards we had between meals?"

"Oh. That was our nourishment."

"Yeah. Yeah. But there wasn't any liquor."

"Everybody needs a rest sometime, Tank."

"Didn't we share the good times, Hardy? And we shared the bad times. That's what makes good friends. Now you're going to sell out."

"How many times do I have to tell you that you're not in touch.

Listen to one who is in touch. Now the city's got a campaign going. They're trying to get to the hard-to-reach. They want to rehabilitate them so that they'll work for their own keep. I happened to be around when a city man was making one of his speeches. You know—being in touch; so I thought I could help clear his conscience and serve my purpose at the same time.

"Look, my friends. We have a little fraternity house. As I said, the winter is getting colder, and a few of our friends froze to death. Remember March. Remember March—the cruelest month. Who wants to leave it up to March whether you live or die?

"Remember Reds? He was sleeping in the doorway across from the park and they set him on fire. And there was another man the week before.

"I'm janitor and keeper of this old shack. And I say that there are those who are master over townhouses and those who are master over shacks."

"See, you thought our clever Hardy had sold out. We've got a place to keep warm."

"You've got a place to keep warm. Now, we have to be discreet about coming and going. If I am found out, then we lose our club house. You won't come all at once. I'll have a signal for you. If I tie back the curtains, you know it's all right to ring the bell. If the windows are covered, then you walk around the block."

"But a man can freeze to death walking around the block."

"You're *used* to walking around the block, Tank. Give a man a taste of something good and he forgets about sacrifice; he's delicate all of a sudden."

"Forget I ever said it, Hardy. Just forget it—you said yourself it was cold outside."

"You got gas, Hardy?"

"You're in touch. We have a gas stove but we don't have anything to cook on it."

"Me and Juice can get some food. We make some pretty regular touches."

"Not Tank *and* Juice, Hardy. We might not see any food."

"You don't trust us."

"I didn't say I didn't trust you."

"Who's talking about distrust? Among friends there is no such thing as distrust. We're all in the same bind. Right? We're in touch with each other. What Elbo means is that we want to choose people with opposite views to take over the food project. That way we don't get anything too wet or too dry."

"What about Stoney?"

"Everybody in favor of Stoney as being co-representative in charge of food appropriation and purchases say 'I.'"

"I."

"All except one—Juice."

"I object because I was insulted. I have my dignity to uphold. There isn't a man here that I couldn't stand beside and be on equal levels with; but you want to say different. I have my dignity."

"The chair recognizes Juice's sense of dignity. All those joining me in such recognition say 'I.'"

"I."

"The 'I's overwhelmingly recognize Juice's dignity."

"Juice can be in charge of supplying the wine cellar."

"Yeah."

"Yeah. Juice can be in charge of the wine cellar."

"Do you mean that? Can I?"

"Yeah. Juice and Spider."

"I nominate Juice and Spider."

"All in favor of Juice and Spider as co-representatives in charge of appropriation for purchases for the wine cellar say 'I.'"

"I."

"The 'I's are overwhelming. Now we need someone to supply literature. We'll want newspapers and magazines—that's part of the keeping in touch."

"I'll watch the baskets. People read on their way to work. They get off the subway at Fifth and that basket's always full in the morning. It wouldn't be any problem."

"All in favor of Slim being in charge of news say 'I.'"

"I."

"Overwhelming."

"Hardy, I have a suggestion."

"Randy has a suggestion."

"I could touch the telephones for extra funds. We could have a jar or something to put them in. That would be for cigarettes."

"Yeah. I'm for that."

"Then what cigarettes we could find on our own as we go along."

"I could touch some of the people living here."

"Sure. They won't mind giving Hardy. He's got something, you know what I mean. When you got something, you can get."

"Yeah. Hardy's got a way."

"He's got a way, all right."

"A way that gets something."

"Now, friends, we know what we promised to do. Remember, we have to be discreet."

"Aren't you allowed to have friends visit, Hardy?"

"You're not ashamed of us—that's not why you want us to be discreet?"

"You don't believe what you're saying, do you? Do you want me to keep this club house or not?"

"What's our coming here got to do with whether you keep it or not? You'll be doing your job, won't you? We won't interfere with what you have to do."

"You tell them, Tony."

"You've got too much character."

"Right, Tony. Who's in favor of making Tony our interpreter, a philosopher in residence?"

"I'm in favor of it."

"All in favor say 'I.' "

"I."

"Overwhelming. And what would you say to Tony helping out when we need extra help in the news, food, and drink department? Is that all right with you, Tony?"

"It's all right with me."

"Yeah. Tony's versatile."

"All in favor of Tony as all-around man say 'I.' "

"I."

"Overwhelming."

"We forgot Elbo. What is Elbo going to do?"

"We don't have a chef."

"Yeah. I'll be chef."

"Everybody in favor of Elbo for chef say 'I.' "

"I."

"Overwhelming. And he can help when somebody needs extra help. Now we've taken care of the preliminaries. Now shall we go on a tour of our club house?

"Two beach chairs, this sofa that opens into a bed. Three lamps. The chimney place. It's not real; it helps make atmosphere. We have a table to sit at and eat our food. A stove with gas for our chef to cook on. A sink with running water."

"What do we need with so many mirrors?"

"We have to keep in touch. But you don't have to look in the mirror if you don't want to."

"How can I avoid it?"

"Well, if you want, we'll black out one of them."

"Who's in favor of blacking out one of the mirrors? All in favor say 'I.' "

"I"

"Overwhelming. Then we'll black out one of the mirrors. Now we'll continue with our tour. Two clothes closets—"

"Who's got clothes?"

"Here's the cupboard—pots and pans, forks and knives. We're in touch. And we've done ourselves proud," Hardy Gallant looking proud.

8

"You're a puritan about work, Nellie. I've learned not to work too hard."

"But, I used to have so much work to do, Miss Watson. It made me feel necessary."

"Yes. You *should* have more responsibility—like being my assistant."

"I didn't mean *that*. I meant I needed more work to keep me busy. I feel wasted just sitting here. I've updated the files and re- placed the supplies. Can you think of anything I can do, Miss Watson?"

"I'll have something for you to do as soon as I can get it organ- ized. Meanwhile, rest yourself," Miss Watson turning away in abrupt dismissal.

Miss Watson does not feel well, Nellie thinking. She was not always abrupt. Perhaps she is pressured with too much work, hav- ing just come back from a trip. But what did she mean when she said that Nellie was a puritan about work? No one works harder than Miss Watson. Perhaps she was trying to put Nellie at ease, stop her from worrying about being idle. Pondering before her desk. She will change the blotter on her desk, wash the desk with soap and water, sharpen the pencils again, wash the telephone receiver. Walking along the corridors to the ladies' lounge, past the painting of "The Last Supper."

"Hi, Nellie. I haven't seen you for a while. You're probably busy in your office; but then, you're always busy. I can tell how busy you are by the papers that come from your office. How do you manage to keep up with so much work? Miss Watson is lucky to have a conscientious worker like you. And she's a nice person to work for. She's a very busy person. She says that you help her a lot, that she doesn't have to worry about a job being finished when she knows you're doing it." Miss Samuels smiling through bifocals. "That's a pretty dress. But you're always wearing something pretty. We were talking about you the other day." Taking off her bifocals to wipe them, putting them on right away.

"I hope you said something good," Nellie smiling and feeling uncomfortable at her staring.

"Yes. All good. We were admiring how well-groomed you are and how efficient. Somebody said that you took pride in doing your work well. Turn around and let me see the dress. Is it warm?"

"Yes. It's wool."

"I was thinking about your knees. Don't they get cold?"

"No." Nellie laughing.

"Oh. Pay no attention to an old lady with arthritis," Miss Samuels reassuringly patting Nellie on the shoulder. "Nice to see you, Nellie. Ask your boss to ring me today sometime."

"I will. Goodbye." Dampening the dust cloth, wetting it and covering it with liquid soap from the dispenser over the sink, something to do until Miss Watson prepares work for her. Miss Watson is pleased with her work, Miss Samuels said. Nellie having heard others say that Miss Watson is pleased with her work. But she has never told Nellie how pleased she is. Nellie creates work when there is no work to do. Nellie not knowing what to do with idleness.

"Hello, Nellie."

"Hi, Cindy."

"I'd like you to meet Timothy. He works here too. We go to the same school."

"How are you, Timothy?"

"Hi."

"Nellie works for Miss Watson, Timothy."

"Oh."

"Don't say 'Oh,' say something," Cindy giggling.

"Where are you working, Timothy?"

"I'm running off the stencils and I'm going to do some of Mr. McIntyre's work. He's going to retire soon."

"That's good, Timothy. I hope your work doesn't interfere with your studies."

"No, ma'm."

"Don't say 'ma'm,' she's not as old as Alma," Cindy giggling, Timothy giggling, too.

"Shouldn't you let me in on the secret? I'm getting a complex."

"We're not laughing at you, Nellie. It's Alma. She's so funny."

"Does Alma know how much she amuses you?"

"You won't *tell* her!"

"Of course not, Cindy."

"We'll be going now, Nellie," Cindy giggling, Timothy giggling, too.

Nellie peering into Miss Watson's office to see if there is work waiting in the work basket on Miss Watson's desk. It is the secretary's duty to lighten the work load of her superior; otherwise, Nellie is of no use. Some letters in unsealed envelopes which Miss Watson has typed. Nellie picking them up.

"Seal those envelopes and mail them, Nellie," without raising her eyes from the papers on which she is writing.

"Why didn't you ask me to type these for you, Miss Watson?"

"You weren't at your desk. I didn't want to bother you; they were rush and I thought I could get them done faster."

"You didn't have to do that, though. I've not worked all morning. I was waiting for something to do. Can I help you with some other work? Perhaps I can organize some of the papers on your desk?"

"No, thanks, Nellie. I know where everything is; but I dropped a report behind the desk—if you'll get it for me—"

Nellie stooping to retrieve the paper, not understanding why she feels undignified about stooping to pick up a piece of paper, placing the paper on Miss Watson's desk and leaving the office. Sealing the envelopes, wondering if Miss Watson remembered to make carbons of the letters and memos so that she can have a record of what she said, stepping to the door. "Miss Watson, did you make carbon copies of these?"

"Carbons?"

"Yes, carbons of the letters you typed."

"It's not important in those cases," looking from Nellie's face downward. Does Miss Watson disapprove of Nellie's knees exposed when hers are so well covered?

"Then I'll put these out for mailing, Miss Watson," Nellie retreating. Washing the desk. The liquid soap creates too much lather on the desk. If Miss Watson were not at her desk, she could apply some of the lather to her desk, too.

Miss Watson coming out of her office, tossing another envolope into the mail basket on Nellie's desk, seeing Nellie washing her desk. "Mine could use a washing, too."

"I can wash yours when I finish."

"No. That's the cleaning woman's job."

"I don't mind. I've always washed my desk."

"But you're not being paid to wash your desk. I'll bet that none of the other secretaries wash their desks."

"I washed my desk because I didn't mind."

"I'm going to write a note to the building supervisor about the floors. They haven't been mopped in some time; and I'll tell them that their people aren't doing their job because my secretary has to wash her desk."

"Hi, Watty. Did your efficient secretary give you my message?" Miss Samuels, bifocals glittering. "I decided to come over and just barge in on you."

"Hi, Sammy. Glad to see you. Come in."

"So you've got Nellie washing desks, now. You slave driver. She doesn't appreciate you, Nellie. Come over and work for me," Miss Samuels chuckling good-humoredly.

Miss Watson looking agitated. "Come on in, Sammy," closing the door.

"Good morning, miss," Charles McIntyre, the office boy, gathering the outgoing letters and memorandums from the desk tray.

"Good morning, Mr. McIntyre," Nellie. "I hear you're going to retire soon."

"Yes, miss. You won't be seeing me after Friday," Charles McIntyre smiling pleasantly.

"We'll miss you. I hope you'll miss us."

"I'll miss you, too, miss. I'll be coming back to visit from time to time."

"What will you do with all of your time?"

"My wife and I have a place in the country. We bought it a few years ago. We knew we would retire some day and we wanted to live in the country, miss. We'll spend some time with the children, too. They're all grown now. Our youngest is thirty. When my wife and I are gone, we'll leave the house for the children."

"That's nice, Mr. McIntyre."

"Yes, miss. My wife and I worked hard and sent the children to college—we have two sons and a daughter; one's a school teacher —our daughter—one son's a doctor, and the other is an accountant."

"I know you're proud of your children, Mr. McIntyre."

"Yes, miss. We're very proud. My wife and I, we didn't get much education; so we wanted to do what we could for our children. We saw that they got an education."

"How long have you been working here, Mr. McIntyre?"

"Twenty-five years, miss."

"Twenty-five years?"

"Yes, miss. My wife and I did catering before that. You're shaking your head, miss?"

"I can't understand how you managed to stay here for twenty-five years—you've been an office boy all of that time?"

"No, miss. I did other things," smiling gently.

"Do you mean—I'm sorry, Mr. McIntyre. I don't mean to be rude, asking so many questions."

"It's all right, miss. It's not so much what you're doing so long as it's honest work. And it's *why* you're doing it, miss. I wish I had more education; but I didn't, so I did the best I could with what I had. You think about why you're doing it, miss. That's what carries you through it. We educated our children so that they could have the chance to choose their work. We, my wife and I, had to make a life, miss. That's what we thought about, making a life. We've done what we wanted, and we're satisfied to rest."

"Mr. McIntyre, I hope you live forever."

"I wouldn't want to live forever, miss. Even old people get tired of sitting. Nice talking to you, miss," Charles McIntyre, strong black face, high cheekbones squaring his face, thin gray mustache, eyes that seem to bear the wisdom for having seen. He might have been chieftain of some order, diplomat. Charles McIntyre, descendant of slaves, no doubt. Charles McIntyre, never having heard of a family tree.

"Ready to go to lunch, Cindy?" Timothy.

"Yes, Timothy, I'm ready for lunch." Giggling because she knows that lunch means sniffing the bottle of correction fluid that she uses to correct her numerous typographical errors. When they are in the corridor, Cindy pulls the small bottle from her purse. "Lunch," laughing, running down the corridor for the fire escape, leaning against the wall, sniffing the liquid.

"Read what it says on the label, Cindy."

"Timothy, you *know* I've read it."

"Then I'll read it: 'Avoid inhaling.' Ha, ha," Timothy inhaling.

"Does it do anything?"

"A little."

"Why are we doing this, Timothy?"

"Because it's forbidden. Ha, ha, ha. It's a farce."

"What is, Timothy?"

"All of it is a farce. They think that by forbidding us they save us. It's your chance to sniff."

"I don't think Alma likes me. She's always glaring at me, and when I speak to her, she pretends not to hear. I heard that she doesn't like young people. Do you know that she won't let me touch the files? She decided that I can't file anything in the right place or that I can't find anything in the files without her help."

"She's just a mean old lady. You ought to give her a sniff of this."

"Timothy, you're so wise."

"Cindy, you're so pretty. You and me, Cindy—we're going to make a beautiful new world. Let's go for a walk."

"Let's, Timothy. Let's go for a walk."

"But can't you transfer her somewhere else? She gets on my nerves."

"What does she do exactly, Alma?"

"She laughs too much. She's not serious about her work. She sits the whole time brushing and feeling her hair. That yellow hair hanging on her shoulders like that. It gets all over everything. Someone ought to make her wear a hairnet. I found some of it in the files."

"She's only part time. I'll see that Cindy stays busy, Alma."

"Oh, Miss Watson. I would have gotten your coffee. I saw you leave the office; but I didn't know it was to get coffee."

"You were busy, Nellie. I didn't want to bother you."

"I wasn't busy. I was talking to Mr. McIntyre. He's retiring."

"Is he?" Miss Watson going toward her office.

"He's an intelligent man, too. Do you know, he's been working here for twenty-five years, Miss Watson."

"Has he? Nellie, empty my desk tray, please. There are some things to be done."

"I'm sorry, Miss Watson. I checked the tray and there was nothing in it." Feeling guilty for having spent valuable time talking, wishing that Miss Watson will continue to talk about something, say anything to break this awful silence while Nellie is gathering the papers from the tray, dropping a letter atop a sheet of paper on which Miss Watson is writing. Miss Watson tolerantly waiting for Nellie to remove the paper, Nellie feeling her tolerance, begging her pardon, rushing toward the door.

"Nellie."

"Yes, Miss Watson," Nellie going to the guillotine.

"Type this up right away. I have to have it in five minutes for a meeting." Still writing, crossing out words, rereading, restructuring, erasing. Nellie waiting, afraid that if she moves she will bring the ax upon her head. She will have to type the letter in four minutes now; three minutes. She will put the paper in the typewriter and type the date, at least. Nellie going toward the door.

"Wait a minute, Nellie."

"Oh. I was going to get the paper ready. You weren't finished." Returning, guilty of assuming what she has no right to assume, waiting, watching. Miss Watson's neck red beneath her bobbed hair.

"Here, Nellie. Do this page. I'll have the rest ready in a while."

The *rest*. Nellie taking the paper. Feeling nervous. Nellie has only three minutes to type. Putting the carbons into the machine. Date. Erasing, discovering that she has put the carbons in backwards, that she will have to begin again.

"Hello, Nellie. I'm back again. Is she here?"

"Come on in, Sammy."

"You are right. She is in. I hear her command," Miss Samuels chuckling, walking into Miss Watson's office.

"Nellie, will you come here, please. Did you finish that page?"

"No, Miss Watson; but I'll be finished in a while."

"Here's the other page. You don't have to make any copies." Staring at Nellie's shoes.

"I bet that dress is new."

"It's not new, Miss Samuels."

"Well, as I said before, it looks nice."

"Thank you, Miss Samuels." Feeling Miss Watson's annoyance, wanting to be gone.

"Do you think it would fit me?" Miss Samuels laughing.

"It should," Nellie blushing.

"She's very diplomatic, isn't she, Watty? I'll never see size twelve again."

Nellie smiling, closing the door behind her.

"I want to say to the dinner guests who have come here in honor of Charles McIntyre, retiring from our midst, that Charles McIntyre is a modest man. So I will make a modest speech to wish him well," Dr. Samuel Lewis, chief executive, looking in the direction of the long table with the white tablecloth, polished silver, gold gilded table settings, where Charles McIntyre, dignified, erect, sits with Mrs. McIntyre, their two sons and daughter.

"Charles McIntyre is ending his twenty-fifth year with us. We have seen his smiling face, heard his pleasant voice for a quarter of a century. Charles McIntyre has never said a harsh word, has never shunned his work, and was always a willing worker.

"He has seen many changes in the twenty-five years that he's worked with us. And the world has changed quite a bit; but through it all, Charles McIntyre has maintained a fine sensitivity and perception. When a man lives through times of rapid change such as we are going through, when a man faces stupendous challenges to his mind and constitution, is a constant target for inhumane acts to his body, spirit, and mind—and when that same man can live through such trials still loving humanity, life, and his work, he is not without wisdom. He is inspired beyond himself. He knows what life is and he knows where compromise begins. He is the wiser knowing where he has been and where he is going because he plowed his way. Bless you, Charles McIntyre."

CHAPTER

9

Harvie stopping to read the menu in the window of The Cafeteria, going inside. He will have roast beef.

Two derelicts sitting at a table stirring sugar into their coffee, one man putting five teaspoonsful of sugar in his cup. He is wearing two overcoats yellow with age and dirt.

Another derelict searching the coin-return slots in the telephone booths, hunting leftover food from tables, finding none.

She has collected the plates, scraped the garbage.

The derelict searching the floor, resigning himself to drinking a glass of water.

Harvie staring at her moving methodically, collecting plates, cups, silverware, wiping away the crumbs, scraping the garbage. The curvature in her back, the corrective shoes, the frail white hands dipping a cloth into a container of water, wringing it.

He is positive that she was born washing tables, clearing away dishes. She has never been an infant, never been young, never done anything but this. Scary. Thinking that she should not be alive at all but for this trifle use, that she should not be missed if she should go away. Harvie thinking of genes. What parentage could have created her whom he feels certain has never been loved, never wanted? She revealing no trace of inner beauty, of inner life; she having no outer beauty, no charm. Scary. Harvie thinking that her life's only meaning is servitude. Wondering why the inequality in the structure of human beings who have nothing to do with the shaping of themselves.

"Watch it, mister!"

Harvie turning, looking after the derelict rushing out of the restaurant with the roll he snatched from Harvie's plate.

"I told you to watch it, mister. You could have grabbed him."

"That's all right. Thanks," smothering his cigarette, getting up to leave.

The traffic policeman blowing his whistle. Traffic is still heavy, the workers trying to get home. Mornings and evenings are the times of day when Harvie is most aware of movement. Harvie feeling the pavement vibrate under the rush of automobiles, of people pushing to get transportation to work, home.

Pretzel vendors pushing their carts homeward. Workers shivering at the bus stop, boarding the bus in a never-ending file, hardly considering their fellows now that the work day is over. Nothing malicious about their shoving; they want to get home to rest before tomorrow. Harvie feeling a heartbeat at his back. Steady, the bus is moving.

Solemn, drawn, sullen, tired faces, going home where they can be moody, quarrelsome, ill company.

A Negro domestic grasping a shopping bag with thick ashen hands the color of earth, hands that no doubt have worked in the potato fields. Harvie feeling guilty for questioning the meaning of his own work when women such as she are hard at work, thinking of work as necessary to living. Thinking of how tired she is, of how much she has done and how much she will be paid. Harvie feeling guilt for despairing that his work is never done. She not minding that the work will never be done. She who would mind if there were no work to be done; for there would be no money to be earned.

Her thin house dress spilling over the side of her seat, she gathering it into orderly folds, tucking it inside her coat, smiling at Harvie caught in her tired glimpse. Her facial features thick and full of pictures. Surely she was one of the women who marched in the army of the dead worker.

Harvie thinking of Essie, the old maid who used to empty the wastebaskets on his last job. Essie, majestic woman of the lower echelon, rough hands fighting through discarded papers, dust and ashes. Essie who used to tell stories about the houses in which she worked before she went to work in the offices, where dirt is a little cleaner. Essie having said goodbye to back doors and freight elevators. Essie having said goodbye to private abuse and come downtown where her former employers' husbands work, used to talk about how one day there would be no more maids. Essie adding that it was too late for her, but in the nick of time for younger generations, laughingly saying that she guessed if she had to lay down the mop then, it would be just the same as dying because she wouldn't know what to do.

The bus pushing out into the din of automobiles lighting their way through the streets, passing on through the night, leaving behind the darkening windows of office buildings, department stores.

Thinking of Nellie blending with a crowd on her way home to cook her dinner; Nellie methodically preparing the meat, vegetables, carefully setting the table with knife, fork, spoon, napkin, and studying the table to see if she has forgotten anything. Then Nellie will eat, wash the dishes, take a book from the shelf and read. So sedate the disposition of women. But Harvie would be pulling up the floor boards, wresting the doors from the hinges. Harvie will telephone Nellie when he gets home.

The bus stops, lets him off amid the familiar surroundings of winter lights. Home again. Pacing, giving Nellie time to get home. Night permeates the apartment, the lights being out. Harvie not wanting lights, wanting to feel the expansion of darkness, lighting a cigarette. Smoking expands his thoughts, though his thoughts aren't new. Taking his harmonica from his pocket, blowing it with a wailing. Harvie needing no tune when all he wants to do is blow.

Nellie ought to be home now. Dialing the telephone, listening to its ring unheeded. Where is she? She ought to be home now.

He will go to the drugstore, get some cigarettes, a way of passing time until Nellie gets home.

The ice-black air growls and growls; the trees like shadows in the night waver under the street lamp. Harvie shivering, hands deep in his pockets. Move on, Harvie Guthrie. Move on.

Sounds sharply scraping against the night. Car doors closing, last summer's leaf scraping the pavement, the lid of a garbage can blown free, a window sash shut tight against the cold. Harvie's shoe soles pounding the ice-cold pavement, the traffic light clicking red, green, go.

Nellie choosing a yellow dress from the better-dress rack of the department store. The mirror tells her that it fits well. Semi-full skirt touching just above her knees, complementing her fleshy legs. The yellow contrasting beautifully with the blackness of her hair. Something new to give her a new feeling, to make new things happen to her.

She will wear the dress from the store. Nellie having nowhere to go. Still, it has been a long time since she has bought a new dress. She has not thought of buying a new dress until now. Nellie works hard to make money. Money is for spending. Nellie deserves something new. No one will see the dress underneath her coat; but Nellie knows she is wearing a new dress. And the thought that something has changed in her life lightens her spirit.

Fifty dollars for a dress that no one will see.

"Going to a party tonight?" the saleslady smiling.

"Yes," Nellie lying.

"You picked the right dress. You'll be the envy of the party. Make the boyfriend jealous."

Nellie smiling.

"Enjoy your dress and come back again."

Nellie nodding, smiling her thanks. She will buy new shoes, gloves, handbag. She working every day for a rainy day, never attending to the everyday. Rainy days wash away. But it is the day unfulfilled that leaves the hunger cramps in the stomach, the convulsions in the heart, that leaves fertile seed to dry in the uterus. Nellie, faithful servant, bedmate . . . *remember her, the dark-haired woman we gave the gold watch to? She was one of our best workers . . . I knew a woman once. Her name was Nellie.*

Trying on new shoes. It has not occurred to her to buy new shoes for the sake of buying new shoes. She has always bought shoes because she needed them. The soft leather shoe feels good, sinks into the thick rug like feet settling on a cloud.

The salesmen are staring at her, following her yellow dress, her quiet movements across the floor, one salesman approaching her.

"May I help you?" The others watching, whispering.

Nellie secretly flattered. "I'll wear them now."

"Yes. Shall I throw these old shoes away, miss?"

"If you'll wrap them, please, I'll carry them."

"Certainly. You have a foot for style. Most women cannot wear that shoe."

"Thank you." Nellie feeling good, knowing that the salesmen are looking at her, feeling pleasantly self-conscious.

She will eat at the Singing Waters Restaurant, order the most unusual dinner, listen to the waterfall, the glasses rattling at the bar. Nellie sliding onto a seat in one of the booths, taking up the dinner menu. Filet of sole and singing water.

"Hello. Nellie. I've been calling you. Where have you been?"

"I've been out, Harvie."

"I know you've been out, but out *where?*"

"What did you want, Harvie?"

"I wanted you to come over."

"What's the matter?"

"I don't know what the matter is. What's the matter with you? Don't you want to come?"

"All right." Sighing. "I'll be there."

Nellie looking into the mirror, combing her hair, touching her brow with pencil, tracing the shape of her lips with lipstick. Feeling newly alive. What do you see in the mirror, Nellie? Hands young and slim, face soft and pretty. You are pretty, Nellie, nothing immodest in knowing. Body young and firm, legs, feet sound and in good reflex. But not forever, Nellie. The body wears and the body tears.

Ringing Harvie's bell, twisting the animated door knob, the buzzing mechanism sounding more like an alarm.

"Nellie." Harvie smiling, taking her coat. "Where did you go tonight?"

"Shopping. I bought a new dress. How do you like it?"

"It's nice. Come here." Taking her in his arms, kissing her.

Freeing herself gently. "What was wrong? You wanted me to come over?"

"I wanted to see you."

"You haven't seen me yet. I told you I'm wearing a new dress and you didn't look at it."

"I said it was pretty. How many times do you want me to tell you?" Kissing her on the neck, ear, hair.

"You're spoiling my hair." Wresting free.

"What's the matter? It's *only* hair. You can comb it. It's not like you to make a fuss about your hair. And why so much attention to your dress? A dress is a dress," taking her into his arms, impatient.

"A dress is not just a dress." Nellie free again.

"Stop that, Nellie. I'm feeling good. Let's not spoil it."

"It's always you. You never think of me."

"I do think of you. I called you, didn't I?"

"You think only of yourself."

"I asked you to stop talking like that, Nellie. I had a rough day."

"I had a rough day, too."

"It's not the same thing. You're—"

"I know. I'm just a woman."

"You're satisfied with your life, Nellie. Women don't have the same needs."

"What needs are they, Harvie?"

"Nellie—"

"What needs, Harvie? We never talk."

"Nellie, don't spoil it. I was so glad to see you. We'll talk some-time, but not now."

"I bought a new dress tonight. I bought new shoes, handbag, gloves; and I went to a restaurant alone because I was tired of the old, tired routine. It was lonely, Harvie. I shouldn't be lonely, Harvie. I'm sick of being lonely. I'm tired of coming when I'm called. Can't you come to me sometime—I'm mad for you, Harvie."

"Nellie—"

"I'm tired of comforting without being comforted. I shouldn't have to comfort myself with a new wardrobe that *I* bought, or with filet of sole that *I* bought. I shouldn't. Tonight I ate at the Singing Waters and I concentrated on the sound of the water to keep from hearing my own tears dropping on my plate. There was so much atmosphere in there, Harvie. Candlelight, wine glasses tinkling. I had a glass of wine, Harvie; and all the time I was drinking I kept looking across the table, wishing that you were there so that I could tell you how warm the wine made me feel, to tell you I was mad for you, to feel you reach for my hand with love for myself, Harvie. Our lives are passing us, Harvie."

"I know, Nellie. Don't you think I know! What can I do about it? What's talking about it going to do?"

"We can build a good life together, Harvie. We could. Our lives could have new meaning."

"Nellie, please. Not now. Why are you so serious all of a sud-den? Cheer up. It wouldn't do for *both* of us to start asking ques-tions about life."

"Because you'd have no one to listen to yours?"

"Nellie, you're unfair."

"You're in a rut; so you use me."

"Stop it, Nellie. Once and for all."

"That's why I bought new clothes. But new things mean only half as much as they could mean if I had someone to share them with. I'm human. I have strong feelings, too. Sometimes I feel like chewing nails, like uprooting things. But I'm only a woman. I'm not supposed to have feelings," swallowing a sob.

"Come here, sweet. I think I love you," kissing her lips.

"Do you understand what I mean?"

"Yes, sweet," kissing her nose, forehead, ears, lips.

"Harvie—"

"Yes, sweet."

"You're not listening. I'm flesh and blood. I feel—"

"Yes. You feel."

"—the same as you feel."

"You feel the same as I feel," her yellow dress soft in his hands.

"*Dead?*"

"Dave, *dead?*"

"Yep."

"Where did you hear that, Jim?"

"Nancy told me. I was the first person she told. I'm surprised she even talked to me. She's front office—Miss Important. Yep. You know I had a feeling that Dave would die. That's why I kept asking about him," Jim faintly smiling.

"Dead."

"Why, we just talked to him. What was it—two days ago, Anne?"

"Day before yesterday."

"Yes, it was." Putting a light to her cigarette, thoughtful.

"You can hold a match to that all day and you wouldn't light it, Sarah. You're trying to light the filter."

"Oh. Thank you, Jim."

"I knew he would die. I was just waiting for somebody to say he died." Jim.

"When did he die, Jim?"

"This morning at six, Nancy said. She ought to know. She's

front office. I wonder if he said anything before he died. Probably not. He never talked much anyway," Jim circling the ash tray with a dead cigarette, blowing smoke. "It's a pity, isn't it, Anne?"

"I should say."

Jim watching Anne's reaction, watching Sarah. "At last he's out of his misery."

"He never said anything about pain."

"But wouldn't you think he'd suffered a lot to have died? There would have to be pain to die. Sure, he suffered," Jim answering his own question.

"Did you hear the news?" Marie from Personnel, standing still in the doorway, no one having heard her arrive.

"Yes. Dave's dead."

"We can't believe it."

"I was telling Sarah and Anne that at least he's out of his misery. He must have suffered something terrible. Did you hear if he suffered? If they were expecting him to die? I imagine it's difficult for his wife. She probably has enough insurance to take care of her and the children and any bills he owed."

"I don't know, Jim. Everyone is contributing money for flowers, Anne. We want to order them today and have them sent to the funeral home. The funeral is day after tomorrow," going out again.

"How much should we give?"

"Marie didn't say how much. I suppose she left it up to us. They'll probably bring a box around. It'll say how much—if there's a certain amount expected from us. Otherwise, we'll give whatever we want."

"I sure would like to know what those big men in the front office will give. I'd give my hat to see what they give. It wouldn't surprise me if they gave nothing at all."

"But they will, Jim. They'll give. You make them seem so un-feeling."

"Why should they? They don't even know we exist. We're not important."

"Then, why are we working? Why are they spending money to keep us here?" Sarah.

"Sarah, you forgot to ask Marie about working part time."

"I couldn't ask her about a thing like that right after the news of Dave's death. How could I ask her, urgent though it is? Anyway, I never thought of it. I'm just surprised that Dave is dead. And he was thinking of coming back to work. He might have died here in the office. He worked late every night." Nodding at Dave's desk, suddenly aware of Harvie rising from his chair, silently leaving the room.

"Do you think our talking about Dave's dying bothered him? He left the room so strangely. As if he thought the chair should be empty. After all, Dave did sit there."

"I don't know, Sarah. He might have gone for a drink of water, or maybe he went to the rest room."

"Yes, maybe he went for a drink of water."

"Anne. Do you know, I didn't see Harvie. When did he come in?"

"He's been here all the time, Jim. He's been working all the time."

"I'm like Jim, Anne. I didn't know he was here until then—until he got up from his chair like a phantom. I thought it was Dave for a minute. Do you know, Anne? I was thinking of Dave."

"Yes, I looked, too, Sarah."

The coffee stains still dyed in the desk. It is not easy to wash away stains of years. Penciled notes where the late David Rock recorded them before they left his memory. The desk calendar holder still empty beside the refill pages for the new year. A black-stemmed smoking pipe dented with teeth marks resting in an ash tray.

Packages of soup crackers in the desk drawer. Half-empty packages of tobacco, pipe cleaners, loose tobacco spilled in the drawers, matches, packets of sugar, adding machine tapes, calling cards from businessmen, phone numbers of office personnel scribbled on sheets of paper. Coffee stains and tobacco grains clinging to the bottom of the wastepaper basket.

The telephone ringing. "Coffee is here."

"Coffee."

"I can use several cups today, Anne."

"I can use a cup or two myself, Sarah."

"Yes. Come on, girls, let's get some coffee. And maybe we can find out more about Dave," Jim.

"So you've come up for air, Harvie," Ferne Darling sharpening the last of several erasers, placing it beside others on the desk, resting her chin on her slim hands.

"Did you know Dave?"

"He passed through now and then, why?"

"He died."

"What a way to end. I knew I had a good excuse for not taking work to heart. Life's for having fun."

"I bet you have lots of fun."

"I make my fun, Harvie. What I can't make, I find. Did you ever hear the story about the cousins? I read it somewhere.

"There were these two cousins, Stephanie and Margaret, whose uncle died and left them a hundred thousand dollars, they being his only living relatives. He was father to Stephanie and uncle to Margaret, who lived with him since the death of Stephanie's mother and Margaret's mother and father.

"One cousin was twenty-five and the other was twenty-eight.

" 'What shall we do with so much money?' Stephanie asked.

" 'I would like to go to Europe and other places,' said Margaret.

" 'Oh, no,' said Stephanie. 'We should use the money more wisely.'

"So they bought a dress shop on the Square. The business grew and grew. A man from South America visited the store and purchased fifty dollars worth of blouses for his women relatives. He was handsome and pleasant, joking with the two cousins. After the man had gone, Margaret said: 'Let's close the dress shop and take a vacation. It would be fun trying on some of our dresses and wearing them to some faraway place.'

" 'No,' said Stephanie. 'We wouldn't have a business when we came back.'

"Twenty years later the cousins had so much money that they did not have to work for the rest of their lives.

" 'Let's sell the store and start enjoying life,' Margaret said. 'We could meet some nice men and marry. It's not too late.'

"Stephanie said: 'How can you talk of selling? Think of what we have put into it. Work is life. Work is why we are where we are today. It's father's work and ours. We cannot simply throw away what we have for frivolity.'

"One night Margaret suffered a heart attack and died. She was sixty-five. Stephanie gave her the largest funeral a cousin ever had and went into seclusion.

"In the spring she asked the authorities if she could remove her cousin's body from its resting place. The body was removed and she went to Europe, where she supervised the burial of Margaret's body. The next year she had Margaret's body removed and traveled with it to South America, where she again had the body interred. The year after, she carried her to the East; and when they had traveled all over the world, Stephanie brought Margaret home to rest, and a year later Stephanie was laid to rest beside her.

"So you see, Harvie, what I'm trying to say."

"It's scary, isn't it?"

"I've got others. Do you want to hear them?"

"You'd better let me digest the one you told. I'm going back to my work. I don't expect to get much work done. So if you see me walking, you'll know it's pretty rough."

"Good luck, Harvie."

A man is dead before he is fulfilled. Life and death are juxtaposed; the difference between the two lies not at their border, but at their extremities. God made man after His own image, and man made things after his concept, needs. The definition of a man is in the way he walks, talks, responds, is responded to, in the work he does. But everything that Harvie does is mechanical, repetitious. The only identification Harvie knows lies in the union label sewn in the lining of his clothing, which he had no part in making.

The lunch hour at the waterfront. The ice-blue air is there, the sun at its apex. Move on. The water's edge, the mud, rotting wood, floating rubble, ships in tow, the sun's reflection riding on the water. Knotting his dexterous hands in his pockets, hot against his thighs. What is the scene that Harvie Guthrie is passing through? Why is he on the scene? The steam passing from his lips says that he is breathing. But breathing is not enough. The ice-blue air is aggressive, pushy. Move on. Only the seaworthy linger here.

David Tyler Rock, husband, father, ardent worker, lying in view at the Neighborhood Funeral Home, his still head slightly elevated above the wooden coffin concealing his body from feet to the waist. The minister praying for the soul of David Tyler Rock. May he rest in peace, now that he cannot know that he rests. The minister never knew David Tyler Rock. David Rock worked hard and slept on Sundays. So the minister delivers the eulogy from fragments of information he has lately come by.

David Tyler Rock, husband, father, veteran of the last war, was a hard-working, gentle, and loyal servant whom the world shall greatly miss. His co-workers at Leslie & Leslie will miss him. You have been faithful, David Tyler Rock. For that, the bleeding heart.

Mrs. Rock weeps. The attendants roll the coffin bearing the remains of David Tyler Rock to her side. Mrs. Rock screams.

His co-workers, Jim Taylor among them, bear the flag-draped coffin to the hearse. David Tyler Rock will be buried in the National Cemetery with fallen fellow soldiers.

The Honor Guard is waiting. The rifle for the salute is ready. The bugle mourns.

Da Da Da—Da Da Da—da da da da da da da da da—Da Da Da—Da Da Da—Da Da Da—

Pop. Pop. Pop.

11

"Anne—"

"Yes, Sarah?"

"Do you believe what Jim said about his fiancée? I mean about half her intestines being taken out. How can a woman work if she's in as bad condition as Jim says she's in, the pain—and how she's not worried. It sounds fantastic, Anne."

"To think about it, it does sound fantastic." Polishing her glasses. "But that's what he said."

"I know, Anne. But it makes you wonder. Besides, I thought he said it was half her stomach that was already missing."

"Oh, Sarah!"

"Well, didn't he?"

"Yes, that's what he said. But that was a while ago. How could a woman go to work every day with half her stomach missing?"

"That's what I'm asking, Anne. How is it possible? Adding to that—rather, subtracting—she is looking forward to having the other half of her intestines removed."

"Sarah. Let's not talk about it." Sighing.

"Still, you can't help thinking. She'd have to be a remarkable woman. That's all I have to say. She's been married before, Jim said; and she has two children, girls, I think. Jim says if anything happens to her, he'll take the children, adopt them. He says he gives her money for them."

"Jim said that? But how can he? He has a mother that he's supporting; and she's not well, at that."

"How can he support so many people on the money he makes?"

"He can't, Sarah. Has he come back from lunch yet?"

"No. But he's due back soon."

"When did Harvie go out?"

"About fifteen minutes before."

"He's not very talkative, is he?"

"It's probably his way, Anne."

"Remember that Jasper? He was a nice fellow, wasn't he? An actor."

"He was nice. He used to tell us stories about his experiences. He finally made it to California. We haven't gotten a letter from him since that first one—when he first left."

"He livened the office. He had a lot of experiences and a lot of jobs. Remember, he drove a taxi at night and sometimes he waited tables? He didn't mind, he said."

"Well, an actor's got to eat, too. He was a little restless, though. He said he wasn't used to sitting so long. Remember how he was up and down, at the water fountain?"

"Yes. And he brought that big thermos of coffee. He liked his coffee."

"He said it helped pass the time."

"Yes. He was nice," Sarah blowing cigarette smoke, reflecting, her brown hair swept to the back of her head in a bun, impeccably groomed, trained to remain intact. Sarah Himes, widow, sole beneficiary of her late husband's legacy.

"Anne, did you hear about the new machine? They're going to install a new machine in that little office where they used to store the records," Jim rushing into the office.

"What kind of machine, Jim?" Anne looking up over her reading glasses.

"It's like a computer. It'll be connected with IYA."

"IYA?"

"Yes. IYA will feed information into it, and it'll be taken off the machine installed here."

"What about the noise, Jim? Won't there be a lot of noise with a big machine like that? How will the people who work near it be able to concentrate?"

"It's not a big computer. It's a little computer. It's wired with the telephone company. I don't know much about it yet, but the front office wants me to spend two days at IYA to learn about the computer. I hear it talks."

"Talks?"

"Yes. You ask it questions and it gives the answers. I'm supposed to find out how it works and then I'll come back and teach you and Sarah."

"But why do we have to learn? That's mechanics."

"Because the front office said so. I guess you should know in case I'm not here one day. It'll be interesting. It's sort of like a teletype machine, they said. They explained it to me in the front office.

"Then I can come back and teach you and Sarah, and I can teach them at the front office, too. I'll be the only one who'll know how to operate the machine. I'll be the only one who'll know what it's about. They'll have to come to me. Can you imagine *me* teaching the big boss? Can you imagine me knowing about the machine and having to teach him because he doesn't know anything about it? They're supposed to know everything."

"Who else is going with you, Jim?"

"I'll be the only one from here. That's what I've been telling you. They chose me to go. If Dave had been here, they would probably have chosen him—no disrespect to the dead. But he had enough on his hands."

"Do you think that's why they're getting a computer, Jim—to do some of the work that Dave did?"

"Well, he's not here. Someone will have to do it," Jim smiling, reddening.

"That's not what I meant, Jim. I mean, do you think they're getting the computer to take off some of the work?"

"I'll be doing the work. I don't know just what—I'll know when I've come back from class."

"Oh. I'll be glad when you find out. I hope it doesn't take you away from your work here too much. That'll get out of hand and we'll have to find somebody to do that," Anne sighing.

"I know. I could work overtime to catch up. They asked me to work last Saturday. They'll probably ask me to work again this Saturday."

"But if they didn't have to take you out of the office when you're needed here, you wouldn't have to work overtime. Besides, you didn't do any of this work when you worked overtime last Saturday, isn't that what you said, Jim?"

"It was some of the work the front office took over when Dave went to the hospital."

"Well, he worked directly with them anyway, so that wasn't working with things from this office, Jim."

"You're right, Anne. You're right. But if Dave had been here, I wouldn't have worked overtime. Did he get overtime when he worked those nights and Saturdays, Anne?"

"I don't think so. He was sort of like an assistant—I don't think he got overtime."

"Do you mean he didn't get paid for working after five?"

"I don't think so, Jim."

"Why did he do it—I mean, what did he get out of doing the work if he didn't get paid?"

"He had a lot of work—a backlog, Jim. He was trying to catch up. I stay a little after five if there's need. It's not that you have to. It's something that needs getting done and he was trying to get it done. That was all. He wouldn't have been doing it all of his life—but just until he caught up. You know how much time he spent with the customers of some of our accounts who had to come in about one thing or another. Now and then it happened like that."

"That's probably why he's dead."

"Jim! He didn't take care of himself, that was it. It doesn't make sense if you're saying that he wouldn't have died had he been paid overtime. He overworked himself, yes. He was a beautiful corpse, wasn't he, Sarah? He looked so peaceful, almost like he was asleep."

"He looked like he was sleeping. He did look peaceful; but not beautiful. Dead is dead."

"Do you think he had enough insurance—I mean, to take care of his wife and children? He didn't have an expensive funeral. You saw the coffin, half closed. They say that kind is the cheapest. She'll get his Social Security, though, and maybe he has army pension. And probably he saved some money. She's probably well provided for."

"I'm sure he wasn't a rich man, Jim."

"But maybe his dying made his wife rich."

"I think he was a man who was careful with what he did with his money. Sometimes he brought his own coffee from home. And sometimes he brought a sandwich and the bouillon. Well, his troubles are over, that's all I can say."

"Yes, Anne," Jim clearing his machine.

"When do you start taking lessons, Jim?"

"Tomorrow."

"Tomorrow?"

"That'll leave only three of us in the office—Sarah, Harvie, and me."

"I know. You know how I feel about leaving you shorthanded, Anne—but it's orders from the front office. Maybe you can get extra help for those two days."

"Marie won't get anybody for only two days—we'll just have to make do. Did you hear that, Sarah, about the machine?"

"I heard. What do you suppose it means?"

"Maybe Leslie & Leslie is thinking of expanding, or something. I don't know."

"Do you think this is a good time for me to press Marie for my shorter day? She might fire me and place a machine at my desk."

"Sarah. I should have known you'd think of something like that," Anne laughing. "And even if that were to happen, they would need someone to operate it."

"Can you imagine me operating a computer—even a baby one that's got connections with the telephone company? I'd be calling the telephone operator to ask her for information. Can you imagine how long Leslie & Leslie would keep me? *Me*, operating a computer. I'll leave that to Jim—Jim can learn. Jim's more mechanical. I like to slide along and take my time. That's why I need that half day. The world's changing too fast for me. Computers and rockets. I want to have time to take my coffee in the morning and hear myself think."

"Sarah, you're funny."

"I don't mean to be. Things change so fast it makes a person dizzy. I'm having enough trouble keeping my feet on the ground with getting old. Trying to keep up with this changing business leaves you feeling like you've been waltzing with a computer."

"Sarah, it's not *that* bad," Anne laughing. "What would you do if things stood still?"

"Well, if things stood still, I'd know whether I was coming or going. But as it is, I have to stay home locked up half a day to find out." Lighting a cigarette, effortlessly putting the lighted cigarette on the ash tray, easing the smoke from her mouth.

"What about your maid? Does she still come to clean once a week, Sarah?"

"Yes. She still comes in once a week. But the work she does hardly makes a difference. She doesn't have to do that much. She doesn't wash or iron clothes. The most she does is dust and operate the electric sweeper, and she mops the kitchen. If I work only half a day from Monday to Friday, I could do the work myself and save that money. I pay her too much for the length of time she's there. They don't work seven-hour days the way we do, Anne. My maid goes home at three; and heaven knows what time she gets there, since I'm not there to know."

"Does she have a key? Is that how she gets in?"

"She has a key. But she's not as bad as the one before. That one didn't get in at all some weeks, and one day she left a note in the refrigerator telling me that she had drunk a can of my beer."

"She had a can of *beer*? *Yours*?"

"Who *else*? It was the only can I had. You know how you'd feel if you went to the refrigerator to get something you know you left there but found a note instead? Anne, I cursed. I read the note and I cursed. What was worse, she thanked me because she drank the only beer I had. Talking of having picnics—she must have had a picnic. I suppose she sipped the beer and watched television as if she was at home in her own living room."

"I've heard that many maids won't work beyond a particular hour, and there's certain work they won't do, and they'll tell you that they don't do it."

"Yes, Anne, and they want the same amount of money for doing less. That's why I'm going to do the work myself. I can do it just as well."

"You can do it, Sarah; you'll have the time when you're working half days."

"I guess I'll go to lunch."

"What will it be today, clam chowder, Sarah?" Jim sucking on a piece of candy. "I've got a lollipop for dessert."

"I don't know if I'll have a lollipop, but I'll have clam chowder."

"There. Didn't I say she'd have clam chowder?" Proudly.

"You remembered that I said El's had clam chowder on Wednesdays and Fridays—and since today is Wednesday—I'll see you later."

"Have a good lunch, Sarah," Jim looking after her, then looking at Anne. "Anne, why does Sarah work at all? She doesn't have to work. She doesn't have to worry about money. Her husband left her well-off."

"Well, Jim, money doesn't last long if it all goes out and none comes in. You know that."

"She'll be able to retire in ten years, and she'll have her Social Security and her husband's."

"Even so, Jim. To have money going out for ten years and none coming in. Ten years is a long time."

"It depends how much money you have. Now I wouldn't last a month. But didn't you hear her say one day that she went singing to the bank? One paycheck doesn't make you sing on the way to the bank. You sing because it's adding up. How many people can deposit their whole paycheck in the bank and not need part of it to pay bills and buy food?

"And she's always talking about stocks and bonds. Do you see her checking the financial pages every day? She doesn't have to work, Anne. If she has stock, she can probably live on the dividends or whatever it is that you get."

"She knows what she has to do, Jim. We're just guessing."

"I'll bet we're close to being right."

"Maybe so, Jim. And then, she might need to work for another reason."

"What other reason than money? Who would work if it weren't for the money?"

"She might just want to keep busy, Jim."

"I can think of better ways to keep busy—working isn't my idea of keeping busy if you have money."

"Even so, there's a drawback to leisure. You can have too much of it, and then money isn't the answer any more. Then money is a problem, because if you didn't have so much you'd be busy working trying to make ends meet."

"Still, I'd like to have the kind of troubles people with money have. Wouldn't you, Anne?"

"Oh, I've got a little nest egg set aside—my husband and I. It's nothing like Sarah, though. I mean, I don't have stocks and bonds. But we're happy. I don't understand anything about stocks and bonds, anyway. If I had them they would cause more headache than not because I'd be worried whether the stock was going to fall, and I'd have to look in the papers, always watching and figuring. Why, I can't figure interest on the nest egg at the bank. I trust the clerks to figure it out. But I don't care about how much interest as much as I care about whether the money I put in the bank is safe and available when I want it.

"Who wants to have so much you have to worry about it and watch it all the time to see whether it's going up or down? And you don't have any control over your investment the way you do at the bank where things just go along no matter what. With stocks you have to worry, worry, worry; and sometimes I think the stocks and bonds are capable of doing some worrying on their

own. If somebody gets sick, the stocks react by falling; if somebody's overjoyed, the stocks rise. If they get an inkling about
something, they react by going up or down, or staying steady—
whatever reaction is appropriate for the occasion. Me, I'll just
keep my nest egg, and all I have to worry about is where I put
the bank book," Anne wiping her reading glasses and chuckling.

"Well, have it your way. But I would trade places with a man
who worried about stocks and bonds any day. I can buy pills for
my worries, Anne," Jim licking his forefinger and flicking the
pages of the papers on his desk.

Harvie standing at the top of the steps, struck still by the echo,
of men and women office workers rushing by him, the purple sun-
set sinking behind the clock tower of another office building.
Lingering at the top of an anthill, skipping the stairs, hands
thrust heavily in his pockets, moving weightlessly among the secretaries, clerks, typists, managers, presidents, vice-presidents;
moving weightlessly because he has no body, only dexterous
hands that want to uproot street lamps, claim them as trophy for
his accomplishment. Harvie Guthrie, hurrah, hurrah.

Sitting in The Cafeteria, eating his dinner, listening to the conversation around him. Pensioned men and retired women dressed
in their best and treating themselves to dinner out. Harvie knows
some of their faces now; they come to The Cafeteria several times
a week. The heavy-set man with the bald head, sleeping with a
glass of water on the table in front of him. And as usual there she
is, moving along pulling the cart full of dishes, silverware, glasses
behind her. How many miles? The bowed apron strings tied behind her back, rigidly dangling as if she moves not at all, accent-
ing the curvature. Her body bereft of rhythm. Only the corrective
shoes and the hands move, not as innovators opening new paths,
but as slaves of habit. How many miles until habit meets full
circle?

12

"We're in touch, friends. We're in touch. Everybody's here," Hardy Gallant sitting in a beach chair. "Juice, Tank, Elbo, Stoney, Spider, Slim, Randy, Tony. Now we'll take inventory of the day's receipts. Who will make the first report?"

"I will, Hardy."

"All right, Randy."

"Sixty cents from the telephone slots in the station. I searched five litter baskets and got a pair of shoes, two pairs of pants, and a coat. That's all."

"Juice?"

"Well, I got two bottles of Fire Ball for the wine cellar."

"Good for you, Juice."

"I didn't get them both, exactly. Spider helped."

"Okay. Juice and Spider."

"The butcher on Delancey Street was throwing this out. It's chopped-up bones; but maybe Elbo can make something with them."

"All right, Stoney."

"I can boil them and make soup, Hardy."

"Good. Elbo our chef says he can make soup for dinner."

"Me and Tank took in three dollars for food appropriations, too."

"Stoney and Tank—three dollars for food appropriations."

"Stoney and Tank can buy two onions. That ought to give the soup some flavor. All in favor say 'I.' "

"I."

"Overwhelming. We're off to a good start."

"Hardy, tell us the truth. How did you get this place? You're not turning citizen on us, are you?"

"*Me*, a citizen? I told you bums. I keep in touch. If I want to stay alive, I've got to be in touch. It's cold outside."

"Hardy's thinking about his future."

"His *future?* Is that why you're doing this, Hardy? You're thinking about your future? What do you want to ruin things for? Why do you want to know about your future? It's better if you don't know; then you don't have to sit around waiting for it to happen."

"Yeah. We're all bums at heart. We have a good life, considering. You don't want to be one of those citizens with expensive cars and houses and bills. You don't want to be one of them who's got everything. Because if you got everything, where're you going, what's to do? But we—we're bums at heart. We got a long way to go—only we take our time, right?"

"Right. What do you want to work for, Hardy?"

"Maybe I'm nostalgic. Maybe I'm celebrating the anniversary of the time I stopped working."

"Yeah, maybe. But you're letting yourself be taken in with this rehabilitating. What you going to do after you're rehabilitated? You going to be some kind of executive? You going from garbage man to executive in some big corporation? That's what you're going to want. You're going to want to graduate to something better and they won't want to let you. You're a bum at heart, Hardy. They don't really want to rehabilitate you. They want to get you out of their eyesight."

"Tony is right, Hardy. You said he was interpreter. It's popular being a bum, Hardy. Look at the Humans."

"They're not bums at heart. They work too hard at it. And they make too much noise."

"They're more frightened than anything; they're afraid that life might come and flatten them—or round them out. But Hardy—you're not afraid. Tell them, Hardy."

"I'm in touch, Tony. To rehabilitate a man, you have to know what he values or valued. In order to find out what a man values, there must be communication."

"What if he don't have no values."

"Every man values something. But if he isn't willing to communicate, to utilize his values—"

"What Hardy means is it's how you make the touch and what you go for that defines you. And if it's a good connection, you make your touch and you pocket it."

"That's a beautiful interpretation, Tony. Somebody's on the bell. Quick! You'd better clear away—the closets!" Hardy cautiously answering the door.

"What's the matter, Hardy? You answer the door like a wanted man."

"Oh, it's you fellows. I forgot you went out. Did you get the onions?"

"Yeah. We brought this, too."

"What is it?"

"Don't tell me you forgot what a tablecloth looks like. We found it in the trash. Wash it off a little and you have something to eat on."

"Stoney, I didn't know you had it in you. You've got some domestic blood."

"Why do you make so much of it? I could have left it where I found it."

"All right. All right. Come on in out of the cold."

"What happened to everybody, Hardy?"

"Let them out. They're in the closet."

"We thought you forgot we were in here. Another five minutes and we'd all be blue."

"We got the onions, Elbo. Do you want us to put them in?"

"I'll put them in. I'm chef. Besides, I have to cut them up first."

"Why do you have to cut them? They'll fall apart when they boil."

"It's the principle. What do you think? I cook slop?"

"We're hungry."

"What's the matter, huh? You see a little bit of food and you complain you're hungry. When you don't have food, you're not hungry. Why? Next, when you get a spoonful in your mouth, you're going to want to eat all of it. What's the matter? You've been going for days without food. Now you can't wait. What do you want—garbage or soup? I don't cook garbage. I cook soup. Garbage, you dump in the pot and let it go. Soup, you make and tend to it."

"What Elbo is saying is—"

"We don't need no interpreter, Tony. We know when we've been bullied. It's the man with the pot that does the bullying every time."

"It's the man with the much-desired pot that does the bullying. Be specific."

"You know what I'm saying. All of a sudden he has big, big power because he's got something we need. It's the same at the mission house. You got to listen to a lot of words as the price of a meal."

"What's that he's putting in the pot? What's that, Elbo?"

"It's seasoning. Why you so particular? You never cared what you were eating before."

"I got the right to know what I'm eating. It's *my* stomach."

"You never thought about rights before. All of a sudden you're thinking about rights. Why don't you set the table and earn your rights."

"It's about time you talked about eating. Where's the plates?"

"No plates, yet, friends. That's another project for us to work on."

"All of us can work on the project. Wherever we find plates, we'll just bring them."

"All in favor of Tank's suggestion say 'I.'"

"I."

"Overwhelming. Now, as soon as Chef Elbo finishes stirring the pot, we'll gather around and eat."

"I'll spread the tablecloth."

"Good. Now, Elbo, you can put the pot in the center of the table—how many spoons?"

"Two spoons is all I can find."

"Well, friends. You heard the inventory on spoons. Shall we make it a community project that each of us be responsible for getting spoons?"

"Yeah."

"All in favor of making spoons a community project say 'I.' "

"I."

"Overwhelming. Now if we'll all gather around the table, Chef will pass the spoon around. But first, with your permission, may I ask Tony to say blessing over the pot?"

"Why? We got it, don't we? So why say blessing? I thought we were done with mission houses."

"I'm not asking that you get religion. It's just a way of keeping in touch. What's wrong with that? You don't have to give up any of the soup and you don't have to feel anything. You don't have to give any more attention to it than you give to the mission house. And we have the choice of not having to hear it at all."

"All right. I got a choice; so say the blessing so we can eat."

"All in favor of saying blessing say 'I.' "

"I."

"Overwhelming. Tony, please say the blessing."

"Lord, thank You for this food. It's not the finest and it's not the most, but we got it. Amen."

"Will you stop that giggling, Cindy!"

"Yes, ma'm. I couldn't help it. You were staring at me."

"You're silly. If you don't come here to act serious, why do you come?" Alma tossing a pencil on the floor. "There's work to be done and you sit there pulling at your hair."

"It was stuck in my collar. I was getting it out," Cindy surprised.

"It's unsanitary. You get hair on everything," Alma blowing her nose and hurrying from the room.

"What did I do?" Cindy to the woman coming into the office.

"I overheard. I'm on the other side of the partition," nodding.

"But what did I do that made her act like that?"

"You didn't do anything. She gets like that sometimes. She's nervous. Just try not to—annoy her—you know, do anything that you think may annoy her—not that you *do* anything—"

"Everything I do annoys her. She just doesn't like me."

"It's not that; sometimes she needs humoring."

"Hi, Cindy," Timothy sticking his head in the door. "Let me take you away from it all." Clowning.

"Take me away," giggling. "Take me away. Away."

"All right. Let's go for a soda. It's time for a break."

"I'll see you later, Cindy," the woman leaving.

"All right."

"Come on. Aren't you thirsty?"

"I'm thirsty. Who's buying?"

"I am. Next time it's your turn."

"Tim—remember I told you that Alma didn't like me?"

"You told me. What's she done?"

"Well, she nearly screamed at me because I was pulling my hair out of my collar. It started when I laughed because she was staring at me. She told me to stop giggling. She's weird."

Laughing.

"She's jealous because you're young and pretty."

"I think she's a sly old lady."

"That's what she is, Cindy. Which flavor will you have—a lime or a lime or a lime?" Pointing to the soda machine designed with selection buttons and a light flashing *Make your selection,* the only flavor being lime.

"Oh, Timothy. I can't make up my mind. You choose," giggling.

"A lime," Timothy pushing the first selection button, "and a lime," pushing the second selection button, "and a lime," pushing the third.

"That's *three* limes, Timothy. Who is the third bottle for?"

"It's for Alma. It's Love Everybody Week. Remember?" Giggling.

"Timothy, I swear!"

"Here," Timothy writing LOVE on a sheet of paper. "Peek and see if she's there."

"Suppose she *is?*"

"Then we'll wait until she goes out again—or you will. She wouldn't take it if you offered it straight out," Timothy giggling, his eyes merry, his dark hair slightly unruly, covering the nape of his neck. "Don't take the top off. She'll think it's poison," giggling.

"Hold mine, and you wait here," Cindy. Timothy nodding and struggling to control the laugh bubbles in his throat.

Timothy playing with the buttons on the machine, watching the light flash on and off. When spring comes, he and Cindy will have vacation from school and work. They will lie on the beach and take in the sun, dip their bare feet in the ocean, chase the waves; and he will teach Cindy to swim.

"She wasn't there, Timothy. She's probably having her coffee."

"What if she doesn't like lime, after all?"

"She likes it, all right. I've seen her drink it."

"Hurry and drink yours. I want you to get back before she gets back. You can see how she acts when she finds it."

"You're smart, Timothy. I'll pretend I'm real busy but I'll be watching her the way she's always watching me."

"What did you do with the 'love' sign?"

"I pasted it on the bottle and I turned it around so she will see it when she sits down."

"Good. You finish. Here. I'll take the bottle."

"See you, Timothy."

Cindy collating the interoffice reports as if she has not been out of the office. Alma walking into the office with weighted footsteps, still clinging to her handkerchief, lowering herself heavily into her chair, looking wearily at Cindy hard at work, looking away, fumbling with papers on her desk. Taking her purse from the drawer, opening it to put the handkerchief in it, changing her mind, returning the purse without handkerchief into the drawer, getting up, pulling out a file drawer, closing it without having looked into it; back to her desk, freezing in front of her chair at the bottle with the LOVE sign; rushing back to the files, furtively looking to see if Cindy is looking.

Cindy is hard at work. Alma tiptoeing back to her desk into her seat, easing the bottle from the desk into the bottom desk drawer, blowing her nose.

"Cindy," gaining her composure. "Who was at my desk?"

"I didn't see anybody at your desk, Alma."

"No one is to fumble at my desk. If they want something, they're to come when I'm here. I can't have my desk upset."

Cindy feeling a giggle rising in her throat, leaving the office before she bursts.

"Are you game, Cindy?"

"Where did you get that? Give it back to whoever you got it from."

"But Cindy, if you try this you won't mind working in the office with Alma."

"That's putting it mildly, Timothy. I may not *know* where I am."

"Isn't that what you want?"

"No. I want to know where I am so that I can protest," giggling.

"What do you think about that suggestion box, Cindy?"

"Oh, *that*. It's a farce. They're just trying to make everybody feel they're having a say about their destiny."

"Let's put a suggestion in the box, Cindy," giggling.

"All right, Timothy. Do you have a suggestion—of course you have a suggestion or you wouldn't have suggested."

"How do you like this: Prospective employees should interview their employers before taking a job."

"Write it down, Timothy. You're so smart."

"We're going to make a new world, Cindy. Come on. Let's put it in the box."

"Yes. Come on, let's put it in the box."

"Wait—you didn't tell me what happened. Did she drink it?"

"Who do you mean? Alma?" Cindy laughing. "No. She got frightened and hid it in her drawer. I think she's saving it."

"Saving it for what? Love in a bottle," Timothy laughing. "Come on, Cindy."

Cindy and Timothy running up the stairs into the corridor.

"What are you two up to?" The receptionist laughing.

"We have a suggestion. Shall I or shall you, Cindy?"

"Let's both of us—let's do it together," shoving it through the perforation, giggling.

"That must be *some* suggestion. Do you want to let me in on the fun?"

"Oh. It's nothing—just a suggestion." Timothy and Cindy laughing, running down the corridor.

"Those two—they certainly have a lot of fun. They remind me of the time when I was young."

"Oh, Elizabeth, you're talking as if you're ancient."

"We won't go into *that*."

"We started working here together, Elizabeth. When was it?"

"Mary, I know I started this, but please, let's not talk about years. If I had my way, I'd stop the clock."

"Wouldn't do any good, Elizabeth. Age is a built-in clock."

"Tell me something I don't know, will you, Mary. Tell me something new."

Timothy walking with Cindy to the office door. "See you at coffee break, Cindy."

Alma dropping the bottle of lime, startled by Cindy's entrance. "Oh! Oh! Why are you always sneaking up like that? What are you up to? Oh!"

"We didn't mean to frighten you, Alma. I'll help you get it up. Did you cut yourself?" Cindy looking at the bits of thick green glass, at the spilled lime, stooping to pick up the piece of paper with LOVE printed on it.

"I'll get it. I said, I'll get it!" Alma retrieving the piece of paper, pushing it into a drawer.

CHAPTER

13

THIS PROGRAM DEMONSTRATES THE POWER OF COMPUTER-AIDED INSTRUCTION TECHNIQUES.

READY GO CARRIAGE RETURN, LINE FEED. Jim striking the keys. ENTER STOCK NUMBER. The machine pounding out the request. 2022020. Jim entering the stock number.

PRE-MIX MARTINIS. . . .

"Pre-mix martinis!" Jim excited. "Did you see that? I'll be!"

INSUFFICIENT STOCK

STOP

PROGRAM REQUEST

"It's fascinating. I've never seen anything like it," Jim to his instructor. "How do you get it to answer like that? I mean, how do you get it to say 'pre-mix martinis'?"

"By programming. You train it to give specific information. This computer was programmed for students. Would you like to try again?"

"Yes. I could do this all day."

READY GO CARRIAGE RETURN, LINE FEED. Jim striking the keys.

ENTER STOCK NUMBER.

2022020. Jim entering the stock number.

PRE-MIX MARTINIS. . . .

INSUFFICIENT STOCK

STOP

PROGRAM REQUEST

"You're doing fine, Jim. Are you getting the idea as to how the computer works?"

"Yes. It's fascinating. The keyboard is something like a typewriter keyboard."

"It gives answers in the fastest time imaginable."

"Can it give more than one answer?"

"There's only one answer. It saves the indecision that might arise if you were forced to choose between alternatives. It has the answer already stored in what you might call its brain, which supplies specific answers to specific questions."

"I'll bet it knows all of the answers. That makes it superior," Jim excited. "And it makes the person who understands it a superior man," Jim reddening.

"All right, Jim. This is how you sign off. Depress that key first."

STOP

"Fine."

PROGRAM REQUEST.

"Now. In answer to the machine's request for a program, you type this":

BYE

"Good. Now watch."

GOODBYE TIME 5:00

"That's fascinating. It's brilliant. It can even say 'bye.'"

"Well, Jim. Here's an instruction manual. You look it over and we'll see you in class tomorrow."

"Bright and early," Jim excited.

"It's so quiet. No one's said a word this morning. Why is everyone so quiet?"

"They're busy doing their work—which is what you ought to be doing, Nancy."

"Oh, Tom. I do my work. You're always saying things like that to me. You can't expect me to come in the morning and start working cold—just like that. I'm not a machine. I can't just take off like that. I've got to collect myself first."

"When are you going to collect yourself, Nancy? You haven't been collected in weeks."

"That's not so, Tom. I don't know why you would say that. Louise can tell you it's not so."

"Are you two at it again?" Louise.

"I'm just telling her. Unless she'd rather Mr. Lewis told her. He's been looking back here quite a lot. He knows Nancy isn't doing as much work as she should. He'll be taking one of his tours."

"Mr. Lewis isn't a policeman. He likes me."

"Don't take it for anything personal, Nancy. He likes production. If you don't produce, the marriage is over."

"Who's talking about marriage?"

"I mean, you're fired if you don't produce."

"Then I'd go to school and study music." Wrapping her fingertips with plastic tape. "I've always had an ear for music anyway."

"I'll bet you've got an ear for listening to your own singing. That's all you've been doing these last weeks—singing about one thing or another."

"He's only kidding you, Nancy," Louise.

"It's not singing anyway," Nancy indignant. "I was born to play the piano. I have an ear for instruments. I never did much about it because I don't feel like going through all the things you have to go through. All the things you have to do to become an artist. It's too much."

"I don't blame you, Nancy. If it's too much, don't do it." Tom winking.

"You're right, Tom. It takes sacrifice. That's right, isn't it, Louise?"

"I couldn't have said it any better, Nancy."

"There, Tom. You heard what Louise said: She couldn't have said it any better. Louise knows." Nancy looking toward the glass enclosure. Mr. Lewis is staring out into space. "Mr. Lewis is always thinking, isn't he, Louise? I guess he has a lot to think

about. I wouldn't want his job. It's too much responsibility. But
Mr. Lewis is a smart man. He wouldn't be boss if he weren't
a smart man."

"I'm sure he wouldn't, Nancy," Louise.

Mr. Lewis reaching for the buzzer on his desk, summoning Mr.
Ames.

Ferne Darling pressing the return key. *F r o s t b u r g ,* Mary-
land. Never mind the frost. Thinking of how near is spring. Ferne
Darling will never work again. She will marry Frederick soon.
She knows how to handle Frederick. Frederick so understanding.
There will be times when she will simply have to fly away and be
what she is. Heaven knows she has her mother's genes. Frederick, believing in the emancipation of women, will understand,
will wait patiently until she flies home in winter. Frederick, house-
warmer, star-struck sentimentalist. Ferne Darling, nature child,
can feel the earth turning. She knows the change. Season and
sensibility.

Autumn touches her in much the same way, fills her with excitement, anticipation of another profound change. Mark how
closely parallel is woman's nature to that other nature, how
closely runs the cycle of her being to the cycle of the seasons.
Ferne Darling determined to get on with her life.

R o c k a w a y B e a c h . Putting the envelope aside. The clock
on the City Hall striking five.

The elevator operator sticking his angel hair out of the door.
"Down." He does not wear the hearing aid. He can relax his ears.
Conveying silence, his nose pointing straight at the door. Down.
Opening the door, bowing and smiling. "Good night. Have a nice
night."

Harvie Guthrie does not want to go home right away. He does
not want to meet the silence just yet. Here he can witness sounds
that come from movement. A balloon peddler punching a large
balloon up into the air, something rattling inside.

Hearing the tapping sound, familiar, irregular in the din of
traffic. The mechanical soldier in the open window of the same
store where Harvie and Hardy watched it on Christmas Eve.

Harvie Guthrie watching it with a new curiosity. What is it about the toy that attracts him to it now? As before, it is its movement. Up and down, around. He doesn't remember what he did with his marching toy. Flicking his burned-out cigarette, walking on, dexterous hands crammed in his pockets. What would he say to Hardy Gallant if he saw him now? Harvie Guthrie doesn't know.

He would feel embarrassed, perhaps. He had all but cried on Hardy's shoulder. He had poured out his troubles to a man he didn't know, had never seen, to a man, no doubt, with greater trouble. What was the truth he hinted at?

"Are you sure you're not wanted for anything, Hardy? Your record's clean with the police and you're not wanted in rogues' gallery?"

"You asked me that before, Mr. Bentley; but I'm not wanted."

"That's good, Hardy. That's good. I don't know why I keep thinking I've seen you before.

"Perhaps you've seen me around here, sir."

"That's it. I suppose. You know I'm going all out for you—if you let me down—

"I don't know why you think I might let you down, sir."

"I'm sorry, Hardy. You've done a fine job here. The tenants have no complaints, and you keep the place clean."

"Thank you, sir."

"We're closing up the place now, and it would be a waste to close you out onto the street again. So I thought you'd like to become a permanent part of our rehabilitation plan. That's why I invited you along. You know, Hardy, this is a great technical age. We're growing by leaps and bounds through technology. Everything will be computerized in a few years."

"Is that good, sir?"

"Of course, it's good. Work will be made easier, faster, and we'll have more time for leisure. Every man will be able to afford leisure."

"But will he know what to do with so much leisure, sir?"

"You ask such strange questions, Hardy. Of course he will. It's his dream."

"*Some* men's dream, sir—if I may say so."

"You surprise me, Hardy. You're a man of leisure, wouldn't you say?"

"I'm a worker in my own fashion."

"I guess you are, Gallant," steering him into a large room full of machines. "Look around you, Gallant. Here we have the greatest problem-solving equipment in the world. If you have a problem and you need an answer, here's where you get it—and faster than man can think. How do you like it, Gallant? You push a few buttons and all of your problems are solved."

"It sounds good, Mr. Bentley."

"Now, Hardy, if you'll take a place among the others, I'll prepare to demonstrate."

Hardy Gallant, hands in pockets, wandering from one machine to another, wondering what it would be like to be locked in a room for a week with these machines, shut off from people, having these machines as sole means of communication. Wanting to keep in touch. What would they say to each other? Hardy being a thinking man.

"May I have your attention, please. I'm Everett Bentley. You're here because you're interested in our rehabilitation program of the future.

"This rehabilitation program is geared toward the training and eventual employment of the so-called hard-to-reach segment of our population. But I say that no man is hard to reach if you offer him alternatives, if you give him room to maneuver.

"Now these are computers, and a part of every man's future. And we want every man to take part in his future, know where he is going and how. To do this, it takes education, motivation, and effort.

"What we're giving you here is a demonstration of the great intelligence of these machines. Let's demonstrate, starting with a subject we're all familiar with—the make-up of our Federal government," Everett Bentley sitting down to a machine.

"Now this machine asks that I enter my name. All right. I'm entering my name: Everett Bentley."

STOP. "It says stop."

PROGRAM REQUEST. "All right. It asks for my request. Watch what happens from here on."

GOVERN. "As you can see, I've chosen government."

READY. "The machine says it's ready."

GO. "All right, it tells me to go; so I'll push the carriage return."

CARRIAGE RETURN

LINE FEED

GOVERN

THIS PROGRAM, USING COMPUTER-AIDED INSTRUCTION TECHNIQUES, WILL TEST YOUR KNOWLEDGE OF THE MAKE-UP OF OUR FEDERAL GOVERNMENT AND REFRESH YOUR MEMORY IF REQUIRED. . . .

RESPOND BY TYPING YOUR ANSWER, FOLLOWED BY RETURN, THEN LINE FEED

INITIALLY, LET'S REVIEW THE BRANCHES OF OUR GOVERNMENT.

"As you no doubt notice while the machine continues to operate, all of these machines have an interconnection. Notice that carbon copies of what the machine is printing here are being produced by the machines on the other side of the room. Hardy, would you like to try this machine?"

"All right, sir." Sitting down to the machine.

READY

GO

CARRIAGE RETURN

LINE FEED

Hardy Gallant picking off the letters: WHAT HAS TECHNOLOGY TO SAY TO MAN'S SOUL?

Rumbling of machines throughout the room, the wild movement of keys making no visible impression on the endless stream of yellow paper pouring out of the machines.

"Push the stop button, Gallant! The machines are jammed!"

STOP—the machine printing on the paper again.

PROGRAM REQUEST. . . .

A DRY MARTINI

"Now do you see why instruction is necessary, why it is a necessary part of our rehabilitation program, for our future growth? Thank you, Gallant, for a good demonstration of what could happen if we don't have the proper orientation."

"I hope I didn't upset anything, sir." Feeling mischievous.

The clock on the City Hall striking six. The once-tight traffic loosened considerably. Policemen still directing traffic. The department stores releasing their workers. Harvie tired of walking nowhere.

There is something in him that wants to happen. Tension that wants exertion. Looking into the window of The Cafeteria, seeing her body bent over a table, wiping, moving on to the next table, the next. How many miles? A nervous quivering in the pit of his stomach, sweat pouring from his armpits. He doesn't know what is happening to him. Turning from the window, waving a taxi. Giving the taxi driver Nellie's address.

"Nellie. I can't breathe," pounding on the windowpane. "I've got to have air."

"I'll open the window, Harvie. You sit down."

"Air!" Driving his fist through the windowpane. Nellie stepping in front of him, catching a wild blow on her head, throwing her arms around him.

"Harvie, *don't*."

Wrapping her in his blood-stained hands, caressing her, ripping at her clothes.

14

"Hi Nellie. Are you busy?"

"Hi Daisy. No, I'm not busy."

"Guess what—I'm going to classes for self-awareness."

"It sounds interesting, Daisy."

"It is interesting." Daisy crossing her arms, caressing her shoulders.

"What is it? Do they teach about how to wear cosmetics and how to dress?"

"No. It's human dynamics. They have classes where I live. They teach you how to bring yourself out. You feel a certain way and you act out those feelings," swaying back and forth. "Life is rhythm. Sedimentation is death, dying," locking her hands under her buttocks and pretending to sit, eyes closed, the brown mole resting on the end of her chin like a stunned housefly, taut, colorless lips, quavering eyeballs that will not go along with the death pretense though her eyelids be closed. Opening her eyes, springing to her feet, smiling. "The rhythm of being. Life is not labor. Life is rhythm." Swaying back and forth. "How did I do? Did I act it out all right? Could you see the rhythm?"

"Yes. That's good, Daisy. That was good acting."

"Did you think so? It's called bringing yourself out. I want to better myself. I'm not good at anything."

"Why do you say that?"

"Some people can do any job well. I can't. I just get by, that's all."

"You like your job in the sales office, don't you?"

"It doesn't have any challenge to it. I need something with a challenge. In the course that I'm studying you learn how to meet challenges. Put your best self forward. Bring yourself out. You know—you keep telling yourself: Life is rhythm. The rhythm of being. Life is not labor. Bring yourself out. I just hope that there's something there to bring out."

"You know there is or you wouldn't be going to the classes. I worked in restaurants so long I thought I couldn't work anywhere else. One day I changed my attitude about what I thought my limitations were and I gave up being a waitress. You grow but you don't always know it until you take a step."

"Did you want to be a secretary, Nellie?"

"Yes. So I went to school."

"I don't know what I want to be. I don't want to do anything special."

"But you're going to school. That means something. You're probably still searching."

"It's a lot of fun. And it's something to do with your time. It saves you from all work and no play. It gives you something to talk about. I met a lot of people—housewives who want to get away from housework. They come; they're older than I am. I'm the only single one, but we have fun."

"Oh—hi, Miss Watson."

"Hello, Daisy. Nice to see you." Miss Watson leaving her office.

"I guess you heard me telling Nellie about school."

"You're going to school," trying to be interested, listening with her eyes tracing the lines on the floor.

"It's a course in human dynamics to bring yourself out," locking her hands together under her buttocks, stooping. "Sedimentation is death, dying," closing her eyes, stiffening her lips, jumping up suddenly. "Life is rhythm," swaying her body. "The rhythm of being. See. That's what we learn. It's something like acting."

"It sounds like an interesting subject, Daisy."

"Oh, it *is*, Miss Watson. I'll go now. See you some other time, Nellie."

"What was that all about, Nellie?"

"She's excited about what she's learning."

"Too bad she's not excited about getting her work done. She could use some tutoring in that," Miss Watson abruptly leaving the office and returning with a dictionary.

"Oh, Miss Watson, you didn't have to borrow a dictionary. I have one here on my desk. And I ordered one for you, too, last year. It's still in your bookstand."

"I didn't see it. I had to look for a word right away and I didn't want to interrupt your conversation with Daisy. She was so carried away with herself," pushing her bobbed hair behind her ears.

"The dictionary was right on my desk. And she would have understood. She wouldn't have thought it an interruption. She knows I'm your secretary."

"She didn't act like it. She acted as if you didn't have anything in the world to do but watch her go through her silly antic. She's getting paid to work."

"She was probably taking her break. She was proud about what she was learning. I'm sorry it bothered you. I'll ask her to speak softly next time, so she won't disturb you—or if you want me to, I'll close the door."

"Nellie, look for my dictionary, please," Miss Watson's neck reddening, abruptly walking into her office.

Miss Watson fingering through the borrowed dictionary. Nellie searching the bookstand, has searched the entire bookstand, looking on the window sill, then searching beneath a pile of papers on Miss Watson's desk.

"Here it is, Miss Watson." Feeling helpful. "You couldn't find it because it was buried under all those papers."

"Oh. Thank you, Nellie. Will you put it on the bookshelf. I'm going to have to clear some of this from my desk. Maybe then I can find things."

"Can I help you clear something, Miss Watson? I don't have anything to do just now."

"No, Nellie. I want to go over them first. You continue with what you were doing." Searching the dictionary.

Nellie leaving, hesitating at her desk, returning to the doorway of Miss Watson's office.

"Miss Watson, Miss Samuels asked me if I could help her office if I had nothing to do. I have nothing to do and you don't have anything for me. I feel that I'm wasting a lot of valuable time just sitting here when I could be doing something."

"Other secretaries have nothing to do. They don't seem to mind."

"I know, but I'd rather be doing something."

"If it's all right with me that you do nothing, then it's no one else's concern. What's wrong with Miss Samuels' secretary? If she can't do the work she ought to hire extra help to catch up." Looking down at the papers on her desk. "Nellie, would you take this dictionary next door, please. I'm finished with it. Where did you put mine?"

"I put it in the bookstand on the first shelf. See. It's the first one with the red cover."

"All right. Return this."

Nellie returning the dictionary, coming back to her desk, standing for a moment, then sitting, thinking. Does she imagine that Miss Watson is cross with her? Nellie does not remember having done anything that would cause Miss Watson to be angry with her.

"Nellie. Will you come here, please."

"Yes, Miss Watson?"

"I dropped an important piece of paper behind the desk; would you get it for me, please. Thank you, Nellie," dismissing her.

Nellie will change the labels on the files and put fresh labels in their place. Nellie opening one of her desk drawers to get the scissors, labels. Nellie having found employment. Measuring, printing carefully.

"Nellie."

"Yes, Miss Watson?"

"Empty the desk tray. I have to get this mail out. And check it more often, please, there may be something urgent in it."

"Yes, Miss Watson. I'm sorry. Shall I make one or two carbons?"

"How many do you usually make, Nellie?" Looking at Nellie's feet.

"You know—the regular two?"

"Then, that's all. Could you type these up right away."

"All right."

"Nellie—just a minute. When you type these, don't erase. These are going to important people and you have to be careful. You've been doing a lot of erasing."

"But sometimes I have to erase."

"If you make a mistake, do it over. It doesn't look good to whoever has to read it, when there's erasing. And it's distracting."

"I'm sorry, Miss Watson. I'll do these right away," Nellie rushing from the office, suddenly succumbing to a fit of tears.

Miss Watson rushing to the door. "What's the matter, Nellie?"

"Why are you punishing me? Why are you punishing me!" Turning abruptly toward Miss Watson, her eyes burning, pain and anger in her voice. "*Why?* What have I ever done to you? Haven't I been a good secretary? You said so yourself. I'm not perfect, but I'm a good worker."

"Nellie, get control of yourself."

"Stop punishing me!" Rushing from the office, down the corridor.

"Why, Nellie. This is a rare visit. All spruced up as usual. Did you come to help me with some work? What's the matter? Tell me." Miss Samuels closing the door when Nellie is in the office. "Sit down, dear. Tell me what's bothering you." Smiling, patting her on the shoulder.

"It's Miss Watson."

"The villain. What has she done?"

"She keeps at me about something. I don't think she's pleased with my work."

"Watty not pleased with *your* work? Why, she's always praising you. Why do you think she's not pleased with your work?"

"She said I make too many erasures. I can't work without erasing. I'll make even more mistakes because I'll be trying hard not to make them. She never said anything about my erasing before."

"Watty is probably in bad humor. She'll get over it."

"But she's getting worse. She acts like she's punishing me for something. You're her friend, do you know what's bothering her? What have I done that she thinks is wrong?"

"Now, I'm sure that a nice girl like you can do nothing wrong. Watty has her problems. Why don't you rest in the lounge. I'll tell her you're not feeling well."

"I think I'd rather go home."

"If you think you'll feel better at home, I can tell her you were too upset."

"Thanks, Miss Samuels. I'll sign out at the desk."

"That's all right, Nellie. You go home and rest yourself."

Nellie trying to smile, nodding to Miss Samuels. Signing out at the desk, pushing aside the employees' suggestion box. *Reason for leaving: Personal.* Taking the elevator down, knowing that she will never return.

"Anne. Do you see how Jim coddles that computer instruction book? He's taken it as his own. Do you see how he locks it in that case of his and takes it home at night?"

"I've seen him, Sarah."

"I think he likes the idea that he is the only one with a copy. He thinks it's his responsibility."

"Yes, Sarah. I think he likes the idea of showing us how the machine works, too.

"That, too. Nobody can deny that. You know, Anne, I think that Jim might have felt neglected one time or another in his life."

"How do you mean, Sarah?"

"Oh, I don't know. The way he acts is part of my reason for saying it."

"Oh, Sarah. There you are again, seeing beyond things. Jim is *Jim*. That's all he is."

"But can't you see, Anne? Why would you have to say that unless there was some special thing that makes Jim *Jim*, as you put it?"

"Sarah, I can hardly keep up with getting the work out, now you're talking about Jim's being neglected."

"Anne, come on. You've noticed him. You're trying to be polite. He's in there now trying that machine, practicing every time he gets a chance. You see him when he comes back, how he puts the instruction book in his case and locks it."

"Yes, Sarah. I've noticed."

"Since all of us have to learn something about it, why don't we take turns reading the instructions—*you* especially, Anne? I'm here only part time."

"Well, Sarah, when the time comes, we'll ask him to lend the book to us, and maybe we could get extra copies. There'll need to be more than one copy anyway. There are the people in the front office who will need copies. And what if the one copy is lost?"

"He won't lose it. You don't think he would *lose* it, do you? He'd probably die rather than lose the book."

"Oh, Sarah. You're so mischievous. Now you're exaggerating. I'm sure there are other things more important to Jim."

"Well, if there are, it's the machine. I think the machine is more important. The only reason he clings to the manual is that it's the key to his learning how the machine operates."

"Then you're wrong about his not wanting to share the book. He's just holding it until he learns everything. Besides, he has to teach everybody else. He has to teach us; so how can he teach us if he doesn't know himself?"

"You're right about that, Anne. But can't you see the feeling of exclusiveness with which he handles the book—like some secret document that only he should know the contents of. He's never let either of us hold the book. He showed us a picture of the machine; but he never let go of the book entirely.

"It's not that I'm over-anxious to learn. You know that. And I'm not talking just to cause an issue, Anne; but the front office expects us to operate it."

"You're right, Sarah. He'll get familiar with it and then he'll show us. He did show us something the first day they installed the machine. I think he was proud to show us and the people from the front office what he had learned."

"He was showing us what he learned; he wasn't teaching us.

That's what I mean. He never gave anybody else a chance to try operating the machine."

"He's been out there long enough. I think he should come in and get some work cleared from his desk. If coffee comes before I get back, please get a cup for me. Black."

"I guess all men are interested in machines, Harvie." Sarah lighting a cigarette, blowing the smoke. "Do you know anything about computers?"

"Not much. I've seen them, but I've not worked with them."

"Are they complicated?"

"Some are more complicated than others, I guess. It depends on what they're programmed to do, I suppose," Harvie lighting a match, coiling his dexterous hands around the flame, putting it to his cigarette.

"I'm not mechanical. My husband wasn't mechanical either. Some people just aren't mechanical," Sarah blowing smoke.

"Women can do other things that men can't do, so they make up for not being mechanical."

"I guess you're right, Harvie."

"Well, here I am, ladies and gents," Jim walking into the office, sitting down. "Anne rescued me. Thank you, Anne. You get so involved with all the things you have to learn and before you know it, you're all done in. Boy, is there a lot to learn. You can sit in there all day and not learn everything. Wait until the real thing starts."

"Do you mean they're not actually using it for business, yet?" Sarah.

"No. That won't happen for a while yet," Jim placing the instruction manual carefully in his attaché case, in the compartment for papers, away from his lunch. "People have to learn to operate it, and there are other things that have to be done. It's a fascinating machine, isn't it, Anne? I was showing Anne how to work it, wasn't I, Anne?"

"Yes."

"Tell her what it said, Anne, when you pressed the wrong key," Jim excitedly.

"You tell her, Jim. You can tell it better than I."

"Well, Anne was supposed to touch one key and she made a mistake and pressed the wrong key; so the machine said: 'Go home and start over again, lump of sugar next time.' Great, isn't it? I'll show you, too, Sarah; but I have to clear the work from my desk. Anne says we're so busy. I guess I'll have to work overtime again this Saturday. Anne?"

"I don't know, Jim. You'll have to ask the front office."

"I'm going to type a note and put it on the machine that nobody is to touch it. I'm the only one who has authority to touch it; and I'm the only one who knows how to use it."

"What makes you think that anyone would touch it?"

"They're a lot of curious people around here. What they wouldn't give to know what I know about that computer. They'd touch it if they get the chance; but they don't know how to get it started, they don't know that you have to say special words to it. I have all of that in my head and in the book."

"Oh, Jim. It's not as complicated as that, is it?" Sarah. "You don't have to know all about how it operates to get *some* response."

"You do with this machine. You have to have the magic words," Jim blushing.

"Then you shouldn't need to put a note out there. If nobody knows the magic words, the machine is safe."

"Still, I'm going to put one on it just to tell them they shouldn't make the attempt—let them know who's in charge," Jim typing the note. "There. *Do not touch this machine. It is not to be played with.* Do you have some sticky tape, Anne? I'm going to make sure it doesn't fall off."

"Here's some," Anne handing him the tape.

"Thanks. I'm going to put this on the machine right away." Rushing out of the office.

Ferne Darling ripping an envelope, dropping it into the wastepaper basket, sharpening the six erasers lying on her desk. It is the third time that she has tried to type the same name and address. Resting her head on the typewriter to pull her mind back into an automatic groove, listening to the clacking of typewriters, listening to Nancy.

"The swelling went down; so I don't have to go to the doctor, Louise."

"Well, that's good, Nancy."

"I didn't smoke much over the weekend. I was a very good girl. It probably wasn't my kidneys after all. It's the smoking, that's what it is. Funny, I never knew that smoking would affect my knees—but you said smoking wouldn't have anything to do with it; didn't you say it wasn't my kidneys, Louise?"

"What did you say, Nancy?"

"You didn't think it had anything to do with smoking."

"I'm not a doctor, Nancy. But, if you're concerned, go to the doctor."

"You're right. That's what doctors are for," Nancy watching Louise, waiting for her to say more and deciding that Louise will say nothing more, fumbling with the papers on her desk. "What you say is true, Louise. Well, I guess I'd better get some work done." Sighing.

Ferne Darling will take a walk to the lounge, indulge herself in a change of scene. But never mind.

The clock on the City Hall striking five.

The clock on the City Hall striking nine.

Ferne Darling walking in the spring air, whistling, feeling the rift between responsibility and frivolity. She would tell the people on the job that this is her last day. No more nine-to-five for her. There's the rest of the world to see. And there is faithful Frederick who is going to marry her for better or for worse.

She will be faithful to him as much as she can. But true marriage is the capitulation of the heart and no matter how many words the minister reads, no matter what blessings he offers to their marriage, Ferne gave her heart long ago.

Frederick has his work. He loves his work. Ferne will have her freedom. Ferne Darling, nature child, has her life in her control.

The air has that something which arouses expectation and it has the scent that Ferne knows from other springs, the subtle fragrance that fills her nostrils with wild notions.

A man in stocking feet is dressing the window of a department store. The buses pulling along beside her, stopping and discharging commuters, and driving away. A bus driver blowing his horn and waving to her. Ferne Darling waving, feeling flirtatious. Spring is no time for rings and things. Spring is the time for flings. The sound of another horn, the driver from the Streets Department wetting down the street. "Don't get wet." Waving.

Stopping at a traffic light, looking at the commuters waiting at the curb, multiplying, anxious to get across the street. She did not braid her hair today; it hangs free. Ferne Darling wanting to linger.

The traffic policeman blowing his whistle, throwing up his hand, indicating that the traffic should stop. Beckoning the traffic with the right-of-way. Proceed.

The blind man out already with his dog and cup. A derelict sitting on the curb tying his shoelace.

Ferne Darling in the lobby of Leslie & Leslie. *"Five?"* The elevator operator, tilting his hearing aid, nodding his white head. "Nice day." Closing the elevator door. "Spring is just about here. *Five.* Have a good day." Opening the elevator door at the fifth floor, bowing.

"This is your last day, Ferne?" Nancy.

"Yes. I won't be back."

"I bet you aren't sorry." Nancy tearing plastic tape and bandaging her fingertips, meticulously, cautiously. "I wish I was going somewhere. Some people are just lucky, I guess. Are you married?"

"Not yet."

"I'm single, too. It's just my mother and me. Where are you going—to another job?"

"I'm going to travel."

"You're going to travel. Louise, did you hear what she said? She's going to travel."

"I overheard. Good luck, Ferne."

"What more luck could she want, Louise? She's going to travel and see things. Me—I guess I'm just stuck here."

"We're slaves, huh Nancy?"

"Slave is the word."

"I think young people ought to do something that's meaningful to them before they settle down to this nine-to-five business day in and day out. If you settle down first, then you may not have the energy later."

"That's me, Louise. That's *me* all around. I settled down first and now I don't have the energy. I wish you good luck, Ferne."

"Thank you." Now that Ferne Darling doesn't have to work she feels that she can work forever. The clock on the City Hall striking five.

CHAPTER

16

Harvie Guthrie taking the back stairway at Leslie & Leslie. The elevator is not running and Harvie does not want to wait. The lights have gone out. Groping his way down the stairway, reaching the landing, lighting a match. Grasping the doorknob, his giant shadow quavering on the door, diminishing with the dying flame. The door won't open.

Lighting another match, climbing the stairs, trying the door on the fifth floor, knocking, down the stairs, up again, stopping at every landing, trying every door. Five again. This is the door through which he came. Turning the doorknob, listening for footsteps, for voices to answer his knock.

"Is anybody there? Open the door!" listening, hearing nothing, sitting on the cold steel steps, lighting a cigarette, staring into the darkness, thinking.

He will try the door on the sixth floor. There is no sixth floor. Knocking on the door again. Today is Friday. If he doesn't get out now, when will he get out? Thinking of starving to death, of smothering to death for want of air. And the darkness. Lighting another match, looking around him wall to wall, his shadow intruding, quavering in the light. Another match gone out.

Sitting on the step again, clamping his dexterous hands together around his knees. Waiting for disaster, the end of the world. Harvie already dead, locked in this mausoleum. Ironic, these stairs. What does a dead man need with stairs when he can go nowhere?

He'd often thought of dying just before his bills were due so that he could escape having to pay them. He had imagined a holocaust that would destroy all record of his indebtedness.

Straining his ears to hear beyond their normal range, getting up, gripping the doorknob, pulling, knocking. He'd better save his energy for the last, conserve himself for the big escape, for the ordeal ahead, or for the last breath when one lived longest in the hope that that would be the moment when one would be saved.

Who entertains the thought of death without contemplating life? Harvie Guthrie wanting life. Lighting another cigarette; the little ball of fire illuminating the end of the cigarette is his company. A couple of inhales and he will put it out. He will have to breathe this same air over and over, better not fill it with too much smoke.

Straining his ears to hear. Tensing his body for a single vibration. Harvie not remembering having witnessed a stillness like this stillness compounded by darkness. Darkness alters perspective, limits one's scope of judgment.

Thinking of Nellie. Is she trapped somewhere in darkness, too? Or is she—God help him if she is dead! Thoughts tapering into sleep . . . into dreaming. . . .

"Your name, please."

"Jeffrey Davidson."

"You're the other partner of Davidson & Davidson?"

"Yes. I'm the other partner of Davidson & Davidson."

"Do you know Harvie Guthrie?"

"Yes. He worked for Davidson & Davidson. I was his immediate superior."

"Then would you say that you are qualified to judge Harvie Guthrie?"

"I am qualified to judge Harvie Guthrie."

"Take your place on the jury, Mr. Davidson."

"And your name is—"

"Anne Bowers. I'm office manager at Leslie & Leslie."

"Do you know Harvie Guthrie?"

"Yes. He works temporarily in my office. They sent him to me from the agency."

"What do you think of Harvie Guthrie, Mrs. Bowers?"

"He doesn't communicate with people. He doesn't have a worker's personality."

"What do you mean by 'worker's personality'?"

"He doesn't act as if he's working with the rest of us—that what he's doing is part of what we're doing. He works apart."

"Take your place on the jury, please, Mrs. Bowers."

"Your name, please."

"Sarah Himes."

"Do you know Harvie Guthrie?"

"Yes. I work with him in the same office with Mrs. Bowers. I work part time; but I used to work full time before I was sick with a cold."

"What do you think of Harvie Guthrie?"

"He doesn't like detective stories. He's snobbish."

"You may take your seat on the jury."

"Your name?"

"James Taylor. They call me Jim. I work in the same office with Harvie and Anne and Sarah. And I'm in charge of the new computer."

"What do you think of Harvie Guthrie, Mr. Taylor?"

"He doesn't like detective stories. He separates himself from us as if he wasn't working in the same office. He's an exhibitionist. He likes to show us how fast he can add."

"All right, Mr. Taylor. Please take your seat on the jury."

"Your name, please?"

"David Tyler Rock."

"Mr. Rock. Do you know Harvie Guthrie?"

"I used to work at Leslie & Leslie with Anne Bowers and James Taylor; but I had to go to the hospital because I became ill with congestion of the chest. Anne Bowers contracted Harvie Guthrie to help at my desk temporarily. They thought I would be coming *back; but I was too sick, and my sickness weakened my body and I died. James Taylor was one of the men from Leslie & Leslie who carried my body after my funeral."*

"James Taylor is a kind man, I am sure, Mr. Rock. It is quite apparent that he, along with your other coworkers, bore you safely to your grave?"

"They did, sir. Thank you for asking."

"Now, David Tyler Rock. What do you think of Harvie, the man who sits in your seat temporarily?"

"Harvie Guthrie does not love work as I loved it. He does not even like it. He doesn't consider it. He does his work without feeling, sir. He is not jealous of his work. He would readily leave it even as he remains in it."

"Do you feel capable of judging him, Mr. Rock?"

"I feel capable of judging, having myself been judged."

"Take your seat on the jury, David Tyler Rock."

"Your name?"

"I wiped his table clean. He smiled at me. I wiped his table clean and he smiled at me."

"You're excused."

"Your name, please?"

"Nellie Worth."

"Do you know Harvie Guthrie?"

"Yes. He depends upon me for love."

"What does he give you, Miss Worth?"

"He doesn't."

"He doesn't give you anything? Are you satisfied with a man who gives you nothing?"

"Perhaps he can't."

"Can't, Miss Worth?"

"I know he should—"

"Would you say that he's all wrapped up in himself, that he has the obsession that he should be served, rather than serve, Miss Worth?"

"I don't know why you say that."

"I haven't said. I'm asking you. Would you say that he uses you, that he does not consider you?"

"But he doesn't think of it that way. He is a good lover. He is going through a bad time now."

"I take it that this bad time doesn't include you."

"I'm trying to understand."

"But isn't it possible to be too understanding, Miss Worth? You might be very old and white before he passes through this bad time you're trying to understand."

"I love him."

"Has this bad time to do with work?"

"Yes. It has something to do with work."

"Do you understand that Harvie Guthrie doesn't like work?"

"Please—"

"Miss Worth, are you capable of judging Harvie Guthrie?"

"I love him."

"You're excused from the jury, Miss Worth."

"Your name, please."

"Ferne Darling."

"Do you know Harvie Guthrie?"

"Yes."

"Did you work in the same place with him?"

"Leslie & Leslie."

"What do you think of him?"

"He's real."

"You're excused, Miss Darling."

"Sir, can you hear me? If not, I can talk louder."

"You asked me something?"

"Can you hear me?"

"Yes."

"Are you acquainted with this man? Do you know him?"

"Do I know him? Yes, I take him up and down on my elevator. I take him up and down, yes."

"What do you think of him?"

"I take him up and down, yes. It's five."

"You may take your seat on the jury. Over there, sir. That's right. Over there."

"Your name, please?"

"Nancy Long."

"*Do you know Harvie Guthrie, Miss Long?*"

"*Yes. He's working temporarily at Leslie & Leslie.*"

"*What do you think of Harvie Guthrie, Miss Long?*"

"*I don't know. He walks with a swagger. But I don't know what to think.*"

"*You may take your seat on the jury, Miss Long.*"

"*Your name?*"

"*Louise Temple.*"

"*Do you know Harvie Guthrie?*"

"*I work at Leslie & Leslie in the same office with Nancy Long. He passes through.*"

"*What do you think of people who pass through?*"

"*I'd say they were irresponsible.*"

"*Thank you, Miss Temple. Take your seat on the jury.*"

"*Your name?*"

"*Marie Hipple.*"

"*Where do you work?*"

"*Leslie & Leslie. I'm in charge of Personnel.*"

"*Then you know Harvie Guthrie?*"

"*Yes.*"

"*What do you think of Harvie Guthrie?*"

"*He seems to prefer his own company. He doesn't communicate with the other workers.*"

"*Now, Miss Hipple, do you have an opening at Leslie?*"

"*Yes. The job at which Harvie is working is open.*"

"*Is Harvie doing the job well?*"

"*Yes. He has marvellous dexterity.*"

"*Has the job been offered to Harvie Guthrie?*"

"*Yes. But he doesn't seem to be interested in work as a long-term occupation.*"

"*Please take your seat on the jury, Miss Hipple.*"

"*May it please the court—*"

"*Who are you?*"

"*My name is Hardy Gallant—defense for the accused.*"

"*If you are the defense, where have you been?*"

"*You see, sir, I had to bum a ride.*"

"*Very well.*"

"Will the prosecution make the opening statement."

"Ladies and gentlemen, the jury is my statement. The jury is the people. I am confident that this jury will convict Harvie Guthrie of dereliction in exercising his God-given talent to work where he is needed, without thought of indulging himself with personal preference for personal satisfaction. Thank you."

"Counsel for the defense—"

"Ladies and gentlemen of the jury, it is nice of you to come. We have to keep in touch. You've gone to a lot of trouble to come here for the sake of this man—all twelve of you, most of whom are known to Harvie Guthrie. If I had a hat, I'd consider taking it off to you for your unusual courage. I have learned to survive by my wits, so I can see that you are already agreed that Harvie Guthrie is guilty."

"Objection!"

"Objection sustained."

"I was merely telling the jury that we are in touch, that it is a no-nonsense jury. Since you are a no-nonsense jury, I am sure that you will not want to carry this trial through a long, drawn-out path to what is already a foregone conclusion."

"Objection."

"Objection sustained."

"What I am saying is that my client wishes to plead guilty and wishes to put himself upon the tolerance of this court. I make a plea for life."

"Harvie Guthrie, will you step forward please. This court is prepared to show you tolerance. What are you giving toward your own defense?"

"My hands, sir. I give you my hands!" . . .

Harvie starting from the steps, eyes aching from their struggle to open to escape from this nightmare. Sweat breaking out on his face. The clock in the City Hall striking five. The lights burning bright. Harvie pounding on the door, running down the steps to the bottom landing, twisting the knob, thrusting the door, sprawling after it, the doorknob strangling in his fist, picking himself from the ground. Angry with himself for having spent the night on a stairway when he could have freed himself.

The clock on the City Hall still striking five. But it cannot be five. The sun is climbing over the rooftops. Automobile traffic is scarce. A man walking toward him, laughing.

"Are you just getting home, too? That was some blackout—electrical power failure. Well, our wives won't be able to quarrel about that."

"No," Harvie trying to conceal surprise, walking on. He will wash his face in The Cafeteria rest room, erase the nightmare from his face. Afterward, he will have a cup of coffee. But first, he will telephone Nellie. Find out that she is all right. What if Nellie should be trapped somewhere? Dialing the telephone, anxious, impatient, waiting for the abrupt end to the ringing and Nellie's voice on the phone. Three, four, five rings.

"Hello."

"Hello—Nellie?"

"Harvie. Where are you?"

"I'm here in the telephone booth."

"I was calling you. I was worried. I thought you might have been hurt or something. Why are you in the phone booth?"

"I didn't get home. I spent the night on the stairs at Leslie & Leslie. I could kick myself."

"Why do you want to say that? It wasn't your fault. Give yourself a break, Harvie."

"I still say I ought to kick myself. I thought I was locked in, only I wasn't."

"Ah, did you?" Nellie laughing.

"Where were you when the lights went out?"

"On the bus coming home."

"That's why you can laugh. I dreamed about you last night, Nellie."

"You called me to tell me you dreamed about me? I thought you called because you were worried about me."

"Why do you want me to be worried about you? You were safe, weren't you?"

"Harvie, I was only kidding. Tell me about your dream."

"You're not interested in my dream."

"I'm interested in your dream, Harvie. But I'm not going to beg you to tell me."

"It was more of a nightmare."

"Then, tell me about your nightmare."

"Why didn't you answer the phone when it rang the first time? Why did you let it ring five times before you picked it up? You knew it was me and you wanted to make me think something had happened to you. That's why you let it ring, isn't it?"

"You're right. I do need someone to worry about me, and I need someone to love me. But I'm not designing enough to play such clever tricks. And how can I be secure with something that I got by trickery? It's the same as not having at all. What do I have?"

"You have me."

"Do I, Harvie?"

"Sure you do."

"I don't have you; you have me. You've always had me. I love you."

"Are you blaming me for that—because you love me?"

"It's not your fault, Harvie."

"But you blame me."

"I don't blame you. You'd love me if you could."

"Is that your clever way of saying that I'm incapable of love? I'm a man, not a monster. You make me sound like a heartless monster."

"We don't share the rhythm, the attunement that two people should share."

"What is this—a piano lesson? Life begins in bedding. Don't deny that; and sometimes that's where it stays if you don't stir it up. Some men can even change life. All I can do is sit in a wooden chair and add numbers on an adding machine, while some clock strikes away my life. I can't move and I can't do anything about it. I don't have any control over my life, Nellie.

"I don't even know what my life is about. Everything is moving so fast, Nellie; I've got to have an equal chance. There's no equality unless you make it. You have to tear down and rebuild. Murder and create."

"Harvie! Don't talk like that."

"I want to be a maker. You're talking about rhythm. *I'm* talking about *thrust*."

"Did you eat breakfast, Harvie? I'm cooking breakfast. That's why I couldn't answer the phone right away. Come eat breakfast. I'll wait."

"If I decide, I'll come. If I'm coming, I'll come. I don't know what I'm going to do."

"All right, Harvie. It's up to you."

Harvie hesitating in the telephone booth, stepping out, lighting a cigarette. Derelicts wandering about. Doesn't like the taste, tossing it into the street. Pondering before the bus stop.

Rhythm—rubbish. Rhythm is Nellie's word. Harvie will have thrust. Harvie craving exhaustion, thrusting his hands into his pockets, fingers coiling into fists, determined against his thighs. Going down to the waterfront.

"What happened?" Harvie Guthrie staring out over the water.

"It's all over. Lot of excitement. See the police boats? They took a woman's body out of the water."

"A woman?"

"Yeah. She was one of them bus girls, you know, that works in the restaurant. She was killed first and then dumped in the river, they say."

"What restaurant?"

"I don't know. It will be in the newspapers. She had a lot of money, maybe. She didn't have nobody, so I guess whoever killed her figured they could get away with it—like she just disappeared."

"Could be."

"But somebody driving past in a car saw a man dump her in the river and they called the police. They just found her. You from around here?"

"No."

"Me either. I just came to watch."

Heavy cargo trucks slowing to watch. Motorists parked near the river. Two nuns pointing toward the river, their black habits fluttering in the wind. Clouds riding high above the gray bridge spanning the river. Yellow, white, red flags waving from wire fencing along the water edge. Two cranes from the dredging company still planted in the water. Smoke rising from smokestacks across the river, fusing with the clouds.

A policeman's whistle blowing the curious drivers on. Make room. Someone is dead, a crime has been committed. Photographers taking pictures. Policemen and detectives writing.

The movement of heavy cargo trucks passing, the street vibrating, the trucks' gears choking. The policeman's whistle. Move on. Hurry. Someone is dead, a crime has been committed.

A derelict warming his hands over a trash barrel glowing with a fire built by workmen of the dredging company. *Miss Florida;* the good ship *Mackintosh* anchored alongside a building, receiving cargo. Several large metal containers marked CARGO waiting for unloading, the scum and debris of the river lurking beside a building. Old netting hanging to the wall of another building. A sign: *Vote—Dedicated Workers Slate.*

A man standing near the trunk of his car parked in the parking lot, pulling on his coveralls over another pair of pants.

A truck unloading in front of the Patterson Seed Company.

The deserted building bearing the name *Brown's Dressed Poultry* gaping at the hollow place left by the demolition men. The weathervane atop one of the shipping houses pointing across the river. The two gray bridges stretching across the river, taking cars over and back.

A siren calling priority of passage for the ambulance bearing the body of the dead woman to the morgue.

Gertrude Swank was her name and she lived in an old house several blocks from the river. Gertrude Swank, daughter of a chambermaid who died a chambermaid, leaving her daughter, Gertrude Swank, the house.

And Gertrude Swank, knowing the cost her mother paid to leave her that legacy, labored to maintain it, though never feeling that it was rightfully hers but that of her mother who labored for it.

She was not attractive, the late Gertrude Swank, having neither good looks nor attractive body. And she was marked with a curvature of the spine and her feet troubled her, so that she had to wear corrective shoes for the miles she walked working as bus girl in The Cafeteria.

She had a voice but seldom spoke to anyone, but she smiled sometimes. She ate all of her meals in The Cafeteria free, ate alone. Gertrude Swank was a loner, walking the six blocks to work in the morning and walking them home at night, forever fearful that one day she might get home to find her house was not in it's place, ever grateful when she found it still remained.

The house was all that she possessed besides the money hidden under the rug, money that was safe as long as the house remained safe.

It cost too much to heat the house with the oil furnace in the cellar, so she kept warm by the little electric stove she bought from one of the second-hand shops on Market Street.

She brought bird seed once a week for Prissy, the little parakeet which kept her company, singing, chirping.

She used to waitress at the counter; but it was observed by the cashier that on several occasions she failed to record all the food she served students who came to The Cafeteria to eat. She not knowing the students personally and the students not knowing her prevented a charge of complicity. Gertrude Swank was becoming fickle-minded, was all they thought.

She had a friend, long deceased, who used to ask her to visit, stay the night, the weekend. But Gertrude Swank kept putting off the visit. She was content to remain at home, although she thought of visiting faraway places.

The house would not be safe if she left it alone. Burglars might come. And who would water the philodendron that she had nourished through the years into flourishing, healthy, green leaves?

And the house would get all musty if it were closed up, the sun would bleach the shades. And she would miss the singing of the birds.

The clock would stop and there would be nobody to wind it.

The telephone would ring and she would not be there to answer it, though it hardly rang when she was at home.

And the money under the rug. What would she do with it until she returned? She could not put it in the bank. They might lose it, or they would not want to give it back when she went to get it, and the government would make her pay tax. So she would stay home to look after her interests each evening, taking care to count the one-hundred-dollar bills, total six thousand dollars.

The restaurant called Gertrude Swank to find out if she was sick, she never having been absent in the fifteen years she worked at The Cafeteria. They sent one of the countermen to her house. The front door was ajar and the rooms in disarray. The parakeet sat petrified on her perch. Gertrude Swank was not at home.

Today, the body recovered from the river is the body of the missing Gertrude Swank. The manager of The Cafeteria Restaurant had the unpleasant task of identifying her body.

Police barricades around the house. Police inside the house, searching, fingerprinting. The parakeet restless in her cage, confused by the new sounds, the new voices. The philodendron green and thriving. The telephone quiet. The money safe under the rug.

"The killer was looking for something."

"Motive—robbery?"

"What was he looking for? Money?"

Gertrude Swank is riding to the morgue. The siren is screaming. Make way for Gertrude Swank.

Harvie Guthrie sitting in the restaurant cafeteria, staring above the cup of coffee hesitating at his lips. For a second he thinks he is seeing her moving among the tables; but no, it is another woman wearing a wedding ring, younger and straight of spine, though round-shouldered.

Taking the hot coffee to his lips at last, feeling the soothing liquid flow down inside him, setting the cup down again, rubbing his hand over the stiff stubble on his face.

Gertrude Swank will never walk here again, will never brush away the crumbs of passing strangers. Furthermore, nobody cares. No doubt the doctors are in the laboratory now, holding her corrective shoes to the light. How many miles, how many miles?

Spreading today's newspaper on the table. He is reading the account of the murder for the fourth time, studying it. Police have found six thousand dollars under a rug in the bedroom of the murdered Gertrude Swank, sixty, an employee of The Cafeteria Restaurant in Center City where she worked as a bus girl. The murderer was probably angered because she would not tell where the money was; so he strangled her, literally broke her neck; then threw her in the river to cover up his crime.

There were scant signs of any struggle put up by the woman, but the house had been ransacked.

Gertrude Swank always walked home. This is the route that she took on the night of her death. Harvie staring at the little map, studying it. This is the way she always walked from her job at The Cafeteria Restaurant, occasionally looking in store windows at things she never bought. What a life she inhabited and not too soon left. Somebody put her out of her misery. The shoes could withstand it. How many miles, how many miles?

Lighting a cigarette, getting up. He has been walking the entire weekend, almost. Back and forth to the waterfront. How many miles?

Walking in the direction that Gertrude Swank followed every day, his dexterous hands squirming in his pockets. The clock on the City Hall striking ten. So definite is the sound of a striking clock, whether appropriate or inappropriate the hour. The traffic policemen are no longer visible, the traffic at even flow. Sunday motorists.

The wind is restless. Move on, Harvie Guthrie. How many miles, how many miles? Time and the machine call the distance. How many miles?

The house is surrounded with barricades. Harvie Guthrie studying the brick row house of the late Gertrude Swank, the drawn green shades, the breathless chimney covered with wild weeds, an ordinary house.

Watching the policemen standing outside the house, talking, guarding. They are not guarding the possessions of Gertrude

Swank, rather they are guarding the evidence of Gertrude Swank. The clutter of furniture, the philodendron, the parakeet, the money underneath the rug. The life savings of Gertrude cost her life, netted her death.

Hands tensely knotted in his pocket, Harvie feeling the pain in his palm, lifting his hands from his pocket, the blood subsiding beneath the skin. A time to murder and recreate. The inequities of humanity. Some people are groomed to excel in all they undertake, are permitted to make a choice as to the work they will do, rake in the spoils, create their leisure. From the beginning of their lives, some people know where they are going, pursuing life jealously, fulfilling every expectation, every endeavor. Why then cannot every person lift himself to an ennobled work, why cannot every man put out his own garbage, bury his own dung, allowing freedom for the noble work?

Gertrude Swank, crumb-scraper, disposer of garbage, who never really was, finally is, will claim her identity with a headstone over her grave, shall be ennobled, until some fool comes through with a plow. So unsentimental some fools that they would wipe out their own basis.

Walking toward the waterfront once more. He must be meticulous. This is the time. He can feel the momentum arising from his intent. Transition. Rebirth.

The two great expansions of bridge stretching across the river. The noon sun casting its white glare over the water. The large cargo trucks passing up and down the streets tremulous under the rolling wheels. Debris in the streets, leaking water from some undercurrent. Men drilling, tearing up a portion of the street.

Looking out over the water to the shore beyond. What do you see, Harvie? Water and land. Water is life flowing out. Land is life come home. You are one of life's ripples flowing at varying levels, intensities.

To some men life takes on meaning, significance, when they forfeit it and then fight to reclaim it. Why did he not think of this before? Harvie shall confess!

Thinking of Nellie. He will confess to Nellie, first. It would be startling to her ears, certainly, but he'd rather she heard it from him than from the newspapers.

Lighting a match, putting it to his cigarette, the wind snatching away the flame, cupping his hand around the cigarette, lighting, inhaling hard, letting the smoke linger in his mouth, wander from his nostrils, then blowing it out of his mouth. Yes. He will tell Nellie. Nellie can take it. And he will love Nellie for the last time in this life. Hastening to Nellie.

CHAPTER

17

"You killed her? You couldn't have killed her, Harvie. What reason would you have to kill her?"

"I killed her to save myself."

"But you couldn't—*save* yourself? From what? Not from her? She couldn't have done any harm."

"She kept mocking me—"

"Mocking you?"

"Yes, mocking me with her presence. Day after day. She just kept scraping those dishes and brushing crumbs as if to say, this is the way your life should go, bend to it or it will break you. She forced me to see the horror of my own life."

"Harvie, it isn't that bad."

"But it *is*. I get up every morning hating it because I know that I will spend the whole day doing work that doesn't mean anything to me. There is no challenge. I'm wasting away."

"You could change jobs."

"Change jobs. It's solved just like *that,* is it? Change jobs and do what? I want to stir up life. Why should work mean survival? Why should it not mean more than that? Why can't work be ennobling? She was an ignoble creature."

"But Harvie—"

"*Ignoble* is the word. She shouldn't have existed in the first place. Those thick hands with big knots on her knuckles, ugly shoes, and she moved like she was already dead. She kept loitering around the dirty dishes as if to say, if I can do this every day without complaining, why should you complain about working with an adding machine? You have it so much easier. You can sit down all day. You make more money and you live better. You have your work and I have mine, and I'm not complaining."

"So you killed her for that? Is that what you want me to believe, Harvie?"

"I told you, Nellie. I followed her home and I killed her."

"I know you, Harvie. You wouldn't kill anybody."

"You *hope* I didn't. For yourself, you hope. If I were a stranger, you wouldn't care whether I killed her or not."

"I love you, Harvie."

"Is that all you have to say to me?"

"What do you want me to say—Harvie, go to the police and tell them the ridiculous story you told me? I love you while I have you, and I'll let you go when I must."

"I don't even own *myself*, Nellie. I don't like myself, so how can you love me? Being in love is for satisfied men. What do you love about me, Nellie? Is it my weakness, my dissatisfaction with myself that makes you love me? You love me because of that? Because it makes me dependent on you?"

"You will not make my love seem like sickness, Harvie. I don't want you to need me. And my loving you doesn't depend on whether or not you love me."

"Then why do you love me?"

"You wouldn't understand, Harvie. You don't love."

"Love isn't everything."

"I never said that it was; but it's all I have. Now you're telling me that you killed an innocent old woman for no reason at all."

"But I gave you the reason; you wouldn't accept it."

"Is it much different from *your* not accepting things? Why should I accept it if I don't believe?"

"Well, you'd better believe it, because I'm going to turn myself in. I came to say goodbye."

"It's a cruel joke, Harvie. It's cruel to put me through this, when you know it isn't true. I knew you didn't love me; but I never thought you hated me. You must hate me deeply to want to make me suffer like this.

"Is there someone else? Then for heaven's sake go to her. But don't put me through this. I'm not holding you. I love you, but that's my fault."

"It hasn't anything to do with you, Nellie. I thought I should tell you first before I told the police, so that you wouldn't be shocked when you read it in the papers. I've got to turn myself in. The sooner I turn myself in to the police, the sooner I can reverse my life."

"*Reverse* your life? Harvie, what are you saying! They'll execute you!"

"It's the chance I'll be taking. Remember what I said about murder and creation? That's what life is—death and creation. Any man deserving to be called a man must write his own saga."

"But you don't have to *prove* anything to *me*, Harvie."

"It's to myself that I need to do the proving. I don't feel like a man who belongs to himself, Nellie—except when I'm with you; but I can't go through my life lying down."

"You're going to give yourself up, have yourself condemned on a lie. Harvie, I'll die. I'll just die."

"Because of me. Nellie, please."

"I'm going to die loving you. You're so complicated, so uneasy to love."

"I never asked you to. I wish you didn't. Nellie, what is it about you? Come closer. This may be our last time." Taking her in his arms.

"Harvie, don't say that!" Locking her arms around his neck.

"Truthfully, it may. We've got to make this last. For all times, Nellie."

"This man says he has a confession."

"What's he confessing?"

"He says that he killed Gertrude Swank."

"What's your name?"

"Harvie Guthrie."

"Now, Mr. Guthrie, you said you killed Gertrude Swank?"

"Yes, I killed her."

"Why didn't you come to us before?"

"I was trying to make up my mind. I was walking, trying to make up my mind."

"So you made up your mind?"

"Yes."

"Why did you kill her?"

"To be rid of her. She wasn't any good—not even to herself. She was just an ugly old woman. She never knew that she was alive, anyway. She never knew what living was. She was too busy working and pinching pennies."

"Did you know Gertrude Swank?"

"Every day I ate at The Cafeteria she was there in her green uniform bending over the tables, brushing crumbs and mocking me with her contentment just to dabble in crumbs, while I was all knotted inside because I wasn't building worlds.

"I wanted to shout: Let them brush away their own crumbs! I wanted to just snatch her away, convince her it was no time for petty crumbs. It's a time of murder and creation, rockets, computers. Life is too quick to waste on petty energies, on dabbling. Get a move on. I wanted to say, How can you bear that static ritual, while machines are running away with your life? Why give attention to crumbs when they're transplanting hearts? I wanted to convince her that she was a victim, that she was suffering and ought to say so.

"I followed her home that night. I pushed her through the door and went in the house behind her. She didn't protest. She looked at me and dropped her eyes and waited. She wouldn't even ask why I was there. 'Do you know why I'm here?' I shouted. She acted almost as if she expected me, and that what happened next was up to me.

"I was angry—her not protesting. If she'd only said *something*—protested life being so hard on her, protested mediocrity, anything; she didn't.

"I grabbed her by the throat to choke one protest from her, a

fight for her life. What is it with you, old mouse? My hands tight-
ened around her throat. What *is* it with you? Can't you even
squeal? Isn't your life worth one protest? Are you going to die
without a fight?

"But she just stared. Then she stopped breathing. She gave up.
The old mouse.

"Did you hear what I said, officer? You're busy writing. I'm telling you why I did it. Listen—it's this—this! Oh damn! She just
gave up—the old mouse."

"Did you rob her? Is that why you followed her home—to rob
her?"

"I didn't want her money. I didn't rob her."

"You didn't touch *anything?*"

"No. I didn't touch anything. I did throw the furniture around.
I was angry. I wasn't looking for anything. She didn't have anything but junk."

"Afterwards, what did you do?"

"I carried her out to the car."

"Is that how you followed her—in the car?"

"Yes."

"You carried her to the car and then—?"

"I put her in the back seat and drove to the river and threw her
in. Somebody heard and I hid myself until they left."

"How do you know that somebody heard you?"

"Somebody blew a horn and stopped; then they drove on."

"What happened to the car you drove to the waterfront?"

"I don't know. I drove a long ways and then I got out and left
it."

"Was it your car?"

"No. It wasn't my car. I saw one at the sidewalk with the keys
in it, so I used it. I think I drove it around the park. I just went
driving. I was confused. I don't know where I left it. All I remember is that I've been walking ever since."

"Check on stolen cars, Frank.

"Mr. Guthrie, you've confessed to a very serious crime—
murder. You're aware of your rights—?"

"I'm aware of my rights. I want to sign a confession. I killed her and I want to sign a confession. I don't need a lawyer. I don't want a lawyer. I'm guilty and I want to be punished. I want to be arrested so that I won't kill anybody else."

"Shall we hold him?"

"Hold him on suspicion of murdering Gertrude Swank."

"Mr. Guthrie—" A policeman leading Harvie into another room. Harvie following. How many miles? You're almost there. His hands dangling quietly at his side, ready to make their print upon the record of their arrest.

Thinking of Nellie, having loved her for the future. I've done it, Nellie. I've given up. Don't cry, and don't wait. Your Harvie has loved you for all times.

18

"Where's Harvie? Has he come in yet?"

"I haven't seen him, Anne. He's late this morning. Monday morning. I think all of us are lucky to even get out of bed on Monday mornings," Jim. "Why is it so hard to get up, especially on Mondays, Anne?"

"I don't know, Jim. It's just hard, that's all."

"Well, I guess after that blackout Friday, everybody is still sleeping to catch up. They say some people were trapped in the elevator between floors here. My girl and I spent the evening in a candle-lit bar."

"How is she mending, Jim?"

"She's all healed up inside. She says she never felt better."

"I guess you and she will be getting married soon."

"Yeah. At the end of the month. We've put it off long enough. My girl is anxious to start building a home for me and the children."

"That's good, Jim. I'm happy for you. But will you have time to get the invitations printed—you're going to have a church wedding, aren't you?"

"Yes. We'll have time."

"You'll have time to make all of the arrangements?"

"We made most of them before my girl went into the hospital."

"Oh. You were smart, Jim. The timing was perfect. How does your mother feel about her son's upcoming marriage? I'll bet she's proud."

"She can't wait. She's very proud. She says she's gaining a daughter and grandchildren all at once," Jim taking the computer instruction manual from his attaché case and putting it under his desk.

"Jim, don't you think you should wait until this afternoon? Harvie isn't in yet, and he hasn't called. He may not come in and I'll be the only one in the office. You know Sarah won't be in until twelve. What you're doing isn't urgent, is it?"

"Well, Anne, it's orders from front office. They want me to learn because I'll have to teach them. You can't fight front office, Anne."

"You said yourself that the machine won't be ready for some time, Jim. I think the work in here is more urgent. You stay at your desk, at least until Sarah comes in this afternoon. I'll take responsibility for delaying your study."

"Front office is your boss, too. They might not like that. They'll think you're trying to go over their authority."

"I don't think so, Jim, once I explain. Besides, they know what our situation is here."

The wedding guests, who are members of the church congregation remaining after the morning worship and strangers to the future bride and groom, are growing restive in their wooden seats.

The ushers conferring. Has the bride arrived yet? She is late by an hour. The pianist and lover of weddings, even though the parties be strangers, will not be able to wait much longer to play the wedding march.

The minister waiting, Bible in hand, to join together James Taylor and Maureen Mullins.

The day began wrong. In the first place, James Taylor forgot to bring their marriage license, which he said Maureen Mullins would be certain to bring when she came. Now Maureen Mullins is late and here he stands among strangers all, excepting Sarah Himes and Anne Bowers sitting out there waiting.

"Where is his mother, Anne?" Sarah Himes leaning forward to get a better view of the front rows.

"I don't know, Sarah. I've never seen his mother. I talked to her over the telephone; but I doubt if she ever knew who I was—my name or anything, unless Jim told her."

"I don't see any of his family—or any of her family, for that matter."

"But I thought you didn't know the family, Sarah."

"I don't know the family, but isn't there supposed to be a certain place reserved for the family?"

"You're right. Perhaps they're going to be late, too."

"*Both* families? What—are they all coming together with the bride?"

"Oh, Sarah, that could be."

"It isn't likely, Anne. I'd say it's not likely."

"Maybe something happened to the bride, the reason why they're late, and the family is helping in some way."

"Still, it's all very strange."

"Maybe the family does not approve. That could be the reason why they are not here. And maybe they are sitting among us."

"Why would they do that?"

"They might prefer it, you know. Besides, Jim's mother is anything but a person of perfect health. She might be sick. But doesn't Jim look nice, Sarah?"

"I think he looks a little ridiculous in that black cutaway and tails."

"Sarah. Why don't we just sit and wait to see what's going to happen. You shouldn't be so critical."

"I don't think anything is going to happen, Anne. We're the only two people dressed for a wedding. Everybody else is part of the morning worship. They probably heard there was going to be a wedding so they're staying to see."

"Well, he sent invitations. He said he sent three hundred invitations."

"Elaborately engraved. But what does that mean if the guests haven't arrived?"

"There's probably a mistake in the time."

"How could there be? The invitation said two. It plainly said two—unless you want to tell me that the rest—the other two hundred and ninety-eight invitations—said four o'clock, because that's what the time is getting to be."

"I hope not, Sarah. The waiting must be embarrassing for Jim, though. What if on the way she had a relapse and had to be taken to the hospital? That would explain why she isn't here."

"Then why hasn't Jim gone out to see where she is, why hasn't he gone to a telephone? He seems content to wait."

"That's hardly fair to say that he's content. You don't expect him to show that he's worried, do you? Everbody else would be worried, and that would cause tension, you know that. That wouldn't be a good atmosphere for a wedding."

"How long should he wait before he decides that maybe something is wrong?"

"Brides-to-be have been late before and so have grooms. That's allowed for. This is just a little longer than usual, I guess, and I can't help feeling embarrassed for Jim. But he'll get over the wait when she gets here.

"Sarah, isn't it wonderful? The expectation makes it even more wonderful, dramatic. Just think how it will be when the pianist begins to play the wedding march and the bride comes through the door. We women are taken so much for granted by our men. I would think that whenever Jim finds himself taking her for granted after they're married, he will remember their wedding day and how long he waited. Then he'll appreciate her all over again as if she was a new bride. He might even consider that she might have come close to not being there at all. If he doesn't appreciate her more after this, then I don't know, Sarah. But he will, and they'll laugh about how she came late to her own wedding."

"Oh, Anne. You're so sentimental."

"There's nothing wrong in being sentimental, Sarah. Being sentimental is what preserves things. It's our foundation. How can we live without being sentimental, without cherishing, without anticipating? That's what makes it all worth waiting for."

"What if that's all it turns out to be—just the waiting?"

"Sarah! You like to tease!"

"Well, I just heard somebody say Jim forgot the license and that she went to get it. Didn't you hear?"

"No, I didn't hear. Who said that?"

"Those people, there. See them? They've lowered their voices. It's four o'clock now. That's two hours we've had to wait, Anne. I haven't had a cigarette in all that time. I'm going out for a cigarette. Do you want to come? Come on; have one too."

"No. I think I'd better wait. One of us should see this wedding. What if the bride comes while you're having the cigarette? Then we'd have missed the wedding. You have one if you want. But maybe you ought not smoke a whole one. We don't want Jim to worry that we've lost patience and gone home. We're the only people from the office, you know. We don't want him to feel we'd let him down."

"Anne, I'm going. I'll be back in time," rising, passing the ushers, out of the door, pulling a cigarette out of her purse. The air is cool and merciful, and the sun is bright and appropriate for a Sunday.

Putting the cigarette between her lips, looking at the discarded church programs lying on the steps, at the families passing by, having left other churches. An usher coming to the church door, stepping outside, lighting a cigarette.

"It's a long wait, isn't it? Are you a friend of the two people who are going to get married?" The usher smiling.

"I work with Jim." Searching her purse for a match, the usher rushing to put a flame to her cigarette.

"Then, you don't know the woman?"

"No. I never met her."

"She sure is giving him a wait. I feel sorry for the man. He must be coming apart inside. You'd never know it, though. He's doing a good job of pretending everything is all right. The man is made of steel. I'd be somewhere looking for her. I wouldn't feel as sure about her showing up as he is. I'd be afraid she'd changed her mind. He must really believe in her greatly to be so sure, to be so patient. The man is remarkable, otherwise I wouldn't be waiting it out with him. I had another engagement at three, but I decided to stay. I admire his courage and patience that much."

"Is this his church?"

"No, he's not a member. I suppose they wanted to be married in church, so he picked this one."

"What about her? Is she a member of this church?"

"No. Neither of them has ever been here before. This is the first time."

"Oh," Sarah puffing her cigarette.

"Excuse me. I'd better get back inside. The bride would be coming upstairs from the basement. You know—from the powder room. Nice talking to you."

Going inside, closing the door.

Sarah Himes tossing away the cigarette butt, brushing the ash from her glove, going inside again. The ushers have left their stations and are congregating in the rear of the church, one disengaging himself from conversation to escort Sarah to her seat, returning again to the conversation.

Jim sitting on the front bench talking to the minister. People in the congregation talking freely.

"What's new, Anne? Something must have happened while I was gone."

"What could have happened, Sarah? Nothing can happen until the bride-to-be gets here."

"Oh, you mean she hasn't arrived yet? I thought she'd arrived."

"Sarah. You know she hasn't arrived."

"Then what's everybody talking about?"

"What would they be talking about? The wedding, about the bride not being here."

"She won't be here."

"Sarah!"

"It must be apparent by now, Anne. Look, the minister is getting up. He's going to say something."

"Friends. May I have your attention. Mr. Taylor wishes me to announce a postponement of the wedding. Something has happened that prevents us from continuing. Mr. Taylor wishes to say something. Mr. Taylor—"

"Friends," Jim red-faced and smiling. "I'm sorry you waited so long and nothing happened."

"What's he smiling about?"

"He's embarrassed. Wouldn't *you* be?"

"—but somehow, I knew this would happen. I prepared myself just in case it happened and it did. We have our disappointments in life; but I'm sorry you had to witness mine. I'm sorry I took your time. But don't be sorry for me."

Eyes of the hushed listeners tearing, staring through the glazed and hushed atmosphere in disbelief.

"Poor man. He's taking it remarkably well. I'd be hidden in the floorboards."

"I wouldn't have said anything to anybody. I'd have left it to the minister. I'd have left by the back door."

"—so if you all want to leave now—"

The minister touching his shoulder. People going up to shake Jim's hand, whispering regret, comforting him. Sarah Himes taking a cigarette from her purse, remembering that she is in church, dropping it into her purse again.

"Anne, do you know, I have the strangest feeling that there never was a bride. It's an eerie feeling—"

"Let me say something to him. Poor Jim. We can't just leave him without saying something to comfort him."

"You go, Anne. I have to have a cigarette. I'll wait for you outside."

"Sarah, I'm surprised at you. I thought you had some feeling. After all, he's just been stood up. I'm sure he must be suffering something awful."

"I have great feeling for dramatic theater, Anne. I've stayed through the show. Now it's over and I'm going for a cigarette."

"Oh!" Anne brushing past Sarah, going to Jim surrounded by sympathetic handshakers and shoulder-patters, touching Jim on the hand. "I know this won't make things all right, but I wanted to say that I'm sorry it turned out so disappointing." Anne.

"Oh, that's all right, Anne. It was bound to happen. I'm glad you came, anyway."

Anne nodding, moving away, making room for others, leaving the church, joining Sarah on the sidewalk studying her new patent leather pumps.

"I just feel so sorry, Sarah. We shouldn't mention this at the office. We shouldn't talk about it to Jim. We'll leave it up to him, if he wants to talk about it."

"I'm sure he won't mind your talking about it, Anne. He needs all of the sympathy he can get."

"But I'm surprised that she didn't come. She didn't seem like the kind of person who would do a thing like that. And Jim seemed to think so much of her. He was good to her. And I should think that if there was going to be any standing up, it would have been Jim standing her up. He's the picture of health who's going to marry a woman with no intestines. She'd only bring him a pile of doctor bills."

"Maybe she never existed."

"What do you mean, Sarah?"

"He never called her by name. He never talked to her on the phone."

"That doesn't mean anything."

"If she'd existed, Jim would have brought her in to show her off. You know how Jim is. Look at the way he is about that machine. He talks about it all day. Look at the way he shows it off to anybody who will look, even if he doesn't want anyone else to operate it. If he was going to marry, he wouldn't let her out of his sight."

"Now, I refuse to believe that, Sarah. He wouldn't go to the trouble of arranging a wedding if there wasn't a bride. That doesn't make sense, no matter how you look at it. If he knew you thought like that he'd be hurt."

"You're not going to *tell* him?"

"Oh, Sarah, even if I believed you, I wouldn't. The clock is striking. What time is it?"

"It's five."

"How do you feel, Jim? Do you feel all right? I was worried about you." Anne. "You said you'd be late. I thought something had happened."

"Good morning, ladies," Jim placing his attaché case on the desk, opening it, taking the computer instruction book from it.

"I guess I shouldn't have worried; you seem in good spirit this morning, Jim. After what happened yesterday, I didn't expect you at all today."

"Oh, that—that's over with. It was for the best, Anne. It was for the best."

"But you must have spent a lot of money—"

"Oh, that. That's the way it goes."

"Haven't you talked to her, Jim?" Sarah.

"No."

"Well, aren't you wondering why she didn't come? Suppose she is sick?"

"She would call me. She hasn't called. Besides, I've changed my mind."

"Well, if you've changed your mind—it's just that you were so eager to marry, Jim."

"Well, Sarah, it's behind me now. That reminds me, did you read this morning's paper about Harvie? Now he says he didn't kill that Gertrude Swank. He says he lied, that he was trying to get involved in something. He got himself *involved*, all right. Murder is involved." Jim reflecting. "You know, I always thought there was something about him, Anne. Didn't you notice?"

"I don't think he killed anybody, Jim."

"He confessed, didn't he? Who would confess if he didn't do it? I knew there was something about him; that's why he was always so quiet. He was plotting then. He didn't want a permanent job because the police might find him."

"He gave himself up, Jim. You have to admit that."

"But now he says he didn't do it. He probably thought he could confess and they'd let him off easy, especially with the reason he gave them for doing it, like he was crazy. How could the woman scream when he had his hands around her neck? You've seen his hands, Anne. They're like a giant's hands."

"Well, he wasn't exactly a *small* man, Jim."

"I know, Sarah. But even at that his hands weren't what I'd call normal. You know, I've always wondered what a murderer was like. I've never met anybody who murdered somebody. You never know. Besides, he knows too much about the woman not to have done it."

"But he said he'd read about it in the paper. He said he studied it over and over until he'd memorized everything."

"But why would he do that? It doesn't sound right. He murdered her. He may fool the police, but he doesn't fool me."

"Jim. The police aren't fooled as easily as you think. They've been trained. All we're going by is our opinion. He was a little eccentric, but that doesn't mean he killed Gertrude Swank."

"Leave it to Anne and she'd free all of the criminals. As far as she'd be concerned, they'd all be eccentric."

"I don't think Anne meant it that way, Jim. I know what she means. He talked to me a little. He seemed all right once he talked."

"Well, it appears that I'm outnumbered," Jim blushing, reaching for the instruction manual. "Time to practice with my little computer." Getting up.

"Jim, didn't they tell you?"

"Didn't *who* tell me what?"

"Didn't the front office tell you about the machine?"

"What about it?"

"Maybe you'd better go to lunch first. Then you can go upstairs and talk to Marie about it."

"Why do I have to talk to Marie?" Clutching the manual, rolling it into a scroll-like shape. "Why can't you tell me?"

"Jim, I think it would be better if Marie told you." Fumbling for her glasses on the desk.

"Why? Am I fired?" Lowering himself into his seat.

"Of course not, Jim. They've called in a job analyst to re-evaluate the working status of the employees. You know, they make recommendations for getting work done more efficiently and smoothly. It has something to do with long-range planning and something they call accountability. Marie can explain it better than I can."

"What's that got to do with me?"

"This analyst—"

"Job consultant, Anne. They're called job consultants."

"I don't know, Sarah. One name is as good as the other. I suppose. They've suggested that Leslie & Leslie hire a specialist—a man who knows everything about computers. It's all going to be computers and there'll be more complicated ones put in, Jim. The man they're hiring will be able to program them."

"They're not going to take my machine."

"Jim, don't feel bad. Just think how much you learned. You might be able to work with him, be his assistant."

"No! They're not going to take my machine. I'm the only one who understands how it works." Grabbing his attaché case, running out of the office into the little room housing the machine, mumbling, "They're not going to take my machine," locking the door.

"Oh, Sarah. I knew I should have followed my thought and let Marie tell him," Anne rushing out of the office, Sarah following her.

"You didn't know he'd take it so hard, Anne. It's not your fault."

Anne turning the doorknob. "It's locked—Jim. Are you in there?"

"They're not going to take my machine."

"Jim. Open the door. You're not acting a bit grown-up about this. Go have a talk with Marie. She can explain it better than I did. And you haven't had your lunch. Have lunch first, you'll feel better."

"I have my lunch. They're not going to take my machine."

"What's the matter with him?" Mr. Lewis rushing to the door.

"He's a little upset. We didn't mean to bother you with it, Mr. Lewis."

"Who is in there?"

"Jim."

"Your Jim?"

"Yes.'

"Jim—Mr. Lewis. Will you open the door, please."

"They're not going to take my machine."

"Call somebody from Maintenance Department, Mrs. Bowers."

"Maybe he'll calm down if we leave him."

"That might be a good idea, Mrs. Himes."

Maintenance repairmen with tools for the lock, setting themselves to the job of opening the door.

"They're not going to take my machine."

The door is open. Jim standing in front of the machine.

"Come on. Let's talk about it in my office." Mr. Lewis.

"No. I can't leave. They're not going to take it," Jim clutching the machine.

"Be gentle. Try not to hurt him."

"Come on, Jim. You don't want to stay here all night, do you?"

"Let go. You can't take my machine. I'm the only one who knows how to use it."

"Come on, Jim boy. We're going to take you home."

CHAPTER

19

"Well, friends, we're going to lose our fraternity house in a few more weeks. But we won't lose touch. We've got to keep in touch."

"Sure, Hardy. We've always kept in touch."

"When do you have to leave, Hardy?"

"Soon."

"We don't need a club house in the spring, Hardy."

"It wasn't so bad, Hardy, us being together. I didn't think I could stand being in a room with a lot of bums."

"Speak for yourself, Elbo."

"You and your lousy cooking."

"That's funny. You never missed a meal."

"Tell him, Elbo. You're not such a bad cook—that's if you can get it down."

"I didn't benefit from eating his garbage. He benefited from me because I helped him believe he was a chef."

"If nobody eats the food, you don't need a chef. Is that what you're trying to say, Stoney?"

"That's right, Tony. Tony's a better interpreter than you are a cook."

"I don't think so. A good interpreter understands *both* sides, don't he, Hardy?"

"A good interpreter has to keep in touch. That's where you find it."

"And Hardy is an interpreter's interpreter."

"You have to pay attention even if you don't want to."

"You're not thinking about rehabilitating, Hardy? I mean, you're not going to give up the good life for a feather bed and a roof? There's nothing like having the stars over your head."

"We ought to make Hardy take a pledge."

"To friends? With friends the very friendship is commitment enough. And then a man owes a pledge to himself, a pledge with which no other man interferes. He keeps in touch with his friends and he shares counsel; but his greatest counsel is with himself. He must be in touch with himself before he gets in touch with others."

"If you say a word to Hardy, he gives you a sermon."

"That's Hardy, all right. We don't want him to preach a sermon, and that's what we'll get without any coaxing."

"You're in touch. You're perceptive, friends. Now shall we have the report of today's transactions? How are the wine appropriations?"

"Me and Juice have one quart for the wine cellar." Spider.

"Good. Now we'll have a report for food. Stoney."

"Pound of dry beans and some bread."

"We could make bean soup—if we only had some soup bones to go with it."

"What do you mean making menus? That's my department."

"He didn't mean any harm, Elbo. Now, we'll have the report on finances—Randy."

"Slow today—only thirty cents. Only three people forgot to take their dimes from the telephone box."

"I've got seventy-five cents from touches."

"And I'd like to tell you that I've been keeping in touch, too. Tips from the house for odd jobs. Five dollars in total."

"I'll bet they were jobs, Hardy. You sure you didn't rob the tenants? It takes hard work to earn five dollars.

"Anchor the man!
Anchor the man!
He'll work himself to death.
Anchor the man!"

"That is a catchy song, fellows. We ought to make it our anthem. Now, what news, Slim?"

"They found the man who murdered that old dame—that Gertrude Swank. Harvie Guthrie—only now he says he didn't kill her."

"Let me see that. Is this his picture? I know him," Hardy Gallant looking at the photograph. "This paper is old. Can't you splurge a little and buy a newspaper? Keeping in touch means keeping in touch with the present, not the past."

"I thought you didn't care so long as it was news."

"I know him. Now, I'll have to go to the library to read the back newspapers."

"I didn't know you went to the library, Hardy."

"How many times have I told you that you've—"

"We know, Hardy. We have to keep in touch."

"Right. A friend's in trouble."

"What are you going to do after you've read all of the newspapers, Hardy? He's not from around here. He's not one of us."

"He's a citizen friend. We made some touches together."

"You and a citizen?"

"Why not? Citizenship is only a matter of acceptance. He was feeling rejected. We were really in touch that Christmas Eve."

"Why we never seen you together, if it was so great?"

"Well, twelve o'clock midnight came and he turned into a citizen again."

"Oh, and then he wouldn't have nothing to do with you and he was filled with shame."

"Nothing like that, friend."

"Hardy just wants to know what happened, that's why he's going to the library."

"I know he's innocent."

"And you're going to prove it?"

"I bet Hardy could."

"I bet Hardy would make a good lawyer for us bums."

"Yeah. They'd get so tired of hearing him preach that they'd throw the case out of court."

"No, friends. That's not the way to win, by tiring people out. How you win a fine and decisive victory is by persuasion. You want the jury to believe every word you say. You want them to accept your logic as their own. You want them shouting in their pews: Innocent! Innocent!"

"Listen. He's talking about pews like he was talking about church."

"I *told* you he's a preacher."

"Now, friends, I've got to go on an urgent mission to the library. Please make yourselves at home; but no small fires, hear? And promise you won't start brawling." Closing the door behind him.

Walking briskly in the direction opposite that of the library, with the old purpose in his step.

"Operator. Person-to-person, collect call to Mr. Bryan Smith; my name is Carl London."

"Ready with your party, Mr. London."

"Hello, Smith."

"Who is this? Is that you, Carl? Carl, where've you been? We've been looking for you everywhere."

"I'm all right, Smith. I'm all right."

"Are you in trouble, Carl? If you are, you've only to ask—but why haven't you called me before now? I was afraid that something might have—"

"Smith, I need your help."

"Anything, Carl. What is it? How are you? What have you been doing with yourself?"

"Thinking. But we'll talk about that later. Can you send me some money. I need a couple hundred."

"Sure, Carl. You tell me where to send it."

"Just send it to the main post office."

"Why the main post office?"

"Are you going to make me sorry I asked for the money because you're asking a lot of questions?"

"All right, Carl. As long as you're not in trouble. You'd tell me if you were in trouble? But I wish you'd come back and begin practicing again. You know I've not taken on another partner, waiting to hear from you, waiting for you to come back. I thought at least you'd have written me to let me know where you were. I know how you felt. But you ought to have stayed and fought."

"How do you fight a prejudice? I'm a man who appeals to reason. I was appealing for a man's right to work. The conditions of his birth were irrelevant. He had no control over his parentage; so why should his choice for a better job be limited for those reasons when he is able to do the work? What's a man to do all his life? Defend his right to work, to live? When will he ever get the time for working, living? A man's work is too much a part of him; and sometimes it's all he has. You know we were right. We were defending the right side and we should have won."

"Right made a good show, Carl; but there are certain realities—"

"You can keep that kind of reality."

"And the way you blamed the jury. It wasn't exactly ethical behavior."

"They were biased from the beginning."

"And your refusing to appear on contempt charges."

"I told them the truth about themselves, and you call it contempt. Anyway, I didn't call you to talk about that, Smith. I've told you what I wanted."

"You'll get it. I don't suppose you know when you're coming home?"

"I don't know, Smith."

"Well, if you're not coming home any time soon, we can arrange to send money every week. I've been making deposits for you in your name. You haven't forgotten what you used to say about allowing money to gather too much dust?"

"No. I haven't forgotten. I'm making another start with my life from the bottom. I've just passed through a phase of life, and I know for the first time the camaraderie of men living on the edge of survival. I have a chance to redeem that failure. I'm going to win this time."

"Carl, you've still got some of the romantic in your blood. I'm older than you are. Every generation has its causes."

"How can you take it so lightly? These are not causes. They're effects."

"That may be true, Carl; but in that same frame lie the realities. Life consists of two marriages. The first time you marry for love. The second time you marry because of the practical and advantageous results that wouldn't be forthcoming if you chose to live outside of the marriage. Once again, I mention the realities."

"I know. I keep in touch—despite my so-called romanticism. Smith, when do you think I can get the money—tomorrow?"

"I'll send it special delivery."

"Thanks, Smith. I'll be in touch—oh, Smith. Address it to Hardy Gallant."

"Why him?"

"We're one and the same."

"You're not in trouble, Carl?"

"I'm not in trouble, Smith. I'm having the experience of my life."

"I've come to the conclusion that you're not going to tell me what you're up to."

"Not right now, Smith. But if I need advice—"

"You'll call me collect if you need anything. Goodbye, Carl."

"I'll be in touch," leaving the telephone booth, rushing to the library, into the Law Department, taking a chair, just sitting among the books and journals. So content feels the man who is on good terms with his work, at harmony with himself. What, indeed, men have to say to each other, they say through their good work.

Taking a law book from the shelf, carefully turning the pages. Hardy Gallant in touch.

20

"Friends, we've been together a long time, and we agree, we've shared the same grass bed and we can trust each other."

"Yeah, that's right, Hardy. Good times."

"And we've had this club house."

"Fraternity house. We like that name better."

"But you know that things aren't always certain with us. One day we're here, and we're somewhere else another day. But we take it in stride because it's the way we've learned to live. We get along and we have nothing to lose."

"What Hardy means is that we're bums at heart."

"That's right, friends. Now in a couple of days I may not be around, and you may even read something about me in the papers. But I want you to trust me. I don't want you to think that I betrayed you, that being your friend was only a game. You're the best friends I've ever had."

"You're making it sound like a funeral, Hardy. Are you in some kind of trouble? You make it sound like we won't see you any more."

"What I'm trying to say is that you may change your opinion of me. You may not feel the same. But however well-intentioned a

166

man's deed, he is bound to alienate himself from one kind of company or another."

"Can't you tell us what it is, why you're going away?"

"No. But I've got a going-away present for all of you. Money."

"Where'd you get it?"

"I got in touch with an old friend. He was feeling generous."

"Hardy's good at that. How much did you touch him for?"

"Enough. I'm going to share it with you and we'll divide the money in the treasury."

"You sure you didn't rob somebody?"

"Hardy is a respectable bum. He wouldn't rob anybody. Besides, when somebody's giving you money, you don't ask where he got it. You take it. You been doing it long enough."

"That's right, Tony."

"What would you say about us having a farewell party? We could have steak for dinner."

"*Steak?* You're kidding!"

"No. I mean it."

"I can't eat steak, Hardy. No teeth."

"We'll get yours ground, Tank."

"All in favor of having steak for dinner say 'I.' "

"I."

"Overwhelming. Now, how's the wine cellar, Juice and Spider?"

"Only half a bottle."

"Well, I'll treat you to the best wine you've tasted in a long time. All in favor—"

"I."

"Well, there's no deliberating on that point. What else can you cook, Elbo?"

"Potatoes, and I can make a salad."

"We don't want no salad. We don't want nothing pretentious. Potatoes and beans, that's what we should have."

"But what about green vegetables? They give you iron, don't they, Hardy?"

"We got enough iron. What you think's been keeping us going? We don't need no green. We need beans. Besides, beans is filling.

You never talked about no green vegetables before. All of a sudden it's so important. I say you're taking advantage."

"It's not taking advantage. It's eating like we should. We may never—"

"That's why we ought to get the beans—to last us in case we *never*."

"All in favor of beans and potatoes with steak say 'I.' "

"I."

"Overwhelming. Now let's see how fast we can have dinner ready. I'm sure we're all very hungry."

"Yeah, Hardy."

"Yeah. Let's go shopping together. That way we know how close we are to eating."

"And *drinking*."

"That's what keeps Tank most happy—drinking."

"All in favor of shopping together say 'I.' "

"I."

"Overwhelming. Now, let's go."

"I'm glad you've expressed your appreciation for Elbo's cooking."

"We always did appreciate Elbo's cooking. We couldn't tell him because he's already got a swelled head."

"All right, Tony will say blessing."

"Lord, thank You for this food, even if it might be the last. Amen."

"Amen."

CHAPTER

21

"Mr. Guthrie, your lawyer is waiting to see you."

"My lawyer?"

"Your lawyer, Mr. Gallant."

"Here I am, Guthrie—it'll take about fifteen minutes, officer."

"Gallant! It's *you*. Is that what you had to say to get to see me?"

"Well, aside from it being true—that is, if you'll let me defend you."

"How did you know I was here?"

"I keep in touch, Guthrie."

"I remember. *I'm* glad to see you again, Gallant. What did you do, borrow a suit to come to see me?"

"If I'm going to be your lawyer, I have to look the part. If you're in touch you'll know that opinions are formed on the basis of appearance, Guthrie. Now, did you kill Gertrude Swank?"

"No. I didn't kill her. Are you really a lawyer? When we met—"

"Let's say I've just come off holiday. I am a real lawyer. Remember I said I lost my job over truth?"

"I remember; but that was all you said."

"I used to think that people responded to truth because it was the highest motivation of response. But that isn't so. People respond to their prejudices and to reality, which isn't always truth.

"Now suppose you *did* kill Gertrude Swank because she was doing mediocre work. Suppose you killed her because she was ugly and useless to everyone including herself, which suggested that even before you killed her she had no life? There was nothing significant about her life, nothing meaningful about it; but she breathed and that is what people take into account. But kill her and the taking of that breath is the reality. No one is concerned with the reason for her death. A reason might lead to exoneration.

"Do you remember where you were the night she was killed?"

"I ate dinner at the restaurant, walked a while, and then I went to see Nellie."

"Nellie?"

"I don't want to involve her in this. I've given her enough trouble."

"If she's a friend, she won't mind helping. And you need help."

"I know. I know."

"Have you seen Nellie since you've been here?"

"No."

"Then you don't know how she feels, whether she thinks you're guilty."

"I told her before I gave myself up that I killed Gertrude Swank."

"Did she believe you?"

"No. She thought I was trying to hurt her."

"Why would she think you'd confess murder to hurt her?"

"She thought I didn't love her and didn't know how else to get rid of her—so if I told her I was a murderer."

"Let's talk to her, Guthrie. We need witnesses for our defense."

"You sure they won't find out you're not a lawyer?"

"I'm a lawyer, Guthrie. Here's my proof."

"Carl London? Is that your real name?"

"That's the real name, Guthrie."

"'The most significant thing about my name is that I named myself'—that's what you said when we met."

"You're in touch, Guthrie."

"What made you take up practice again?"

"You."

"I don't know why."

"You and I are philosophers, Harvie. You've created a challenge for me. I'm not only defending a man this time. I'm defending the embodiment of truth. One usually calls to mind an intangible called truth and tries to apply it by argument or by example to a discourse or deed. You're the tangible truth of man fighting against dehumanization by a rampant technological, mechanical civilization."

"Well, whatever your reason, it isn't money because you know I don't have money."

"You're perceptive, Guthrie. What about that uptown place? Do you still have it?"

"I may not have it long."

"So you never got rid of it? But you've got bigger matters to worry about—matters of life. Now Guthrie, you try not to worry and trust me."

"If, when you talk to Nellie, she'll come to see me—you don't need to say I told you to ask her. Just suggest it and see how she takes the idea."

"I understand, Guthrie. I'm in touch. I'll be seeing you soon."

22

Harvie Guthrie working in the stone quarry, gathering the smaller pieces blasted from the earth. Holding a piece of stone, cool, solid in the palm of his hands.

Thinking of Gertrude Swank. With this stone, with these hands, he can carve a monument for her grave; better yet, a monument to all the workers.

"What's wrong with it, Guthrie?" A prison guard calling.

"Nothing."

"Let's get it loaded."

Tossing stone on stone into the truck, feeling the muscles in his shoulders, arms, back, feeling his whole body put to use, alive. Feeling glad that he is allowed to work here until his trial, wondering at the feeling of accomplishment as he tosses another rock into the truck. Stone is for building.

The warning whistle. Below, men preparing to blast more stone. Beyond the stone lies water, still and deep.

When Harvie Guthrie is free again, and he will be free, being innocent, Harvie will go to work in a stone quarry. Harvie Guthrie, earth mover. He will work in the quarry by day and by night he will build monuments of stone that will lend tribute to the workers, living and dead. Looking at his hands, large and nimble, dexterous, slightly calloused now by his new work, having found this work compatible to his hands.

He will ask permission to keep a large piece of stone. Perhaps the prison will allow him to work in the workshop. He will build a monument to all the Gertrude Swanks. He will build a monument to all the workers, title it "The Workers." This will be Harvie Guthrie's penance, his tribute.

"Let's get it loaded, Guthrie. Is something wrong with your hands? Did you cut them?"

"It's all right." Wiping the blood from the stone, tossing it onto the truck. "My hands will get used to it."

"Hello, Harvie." Searching his face through the lace separation between them.

"Hello, Nellie. You came to see me."

"You didn't want me to?"

"I'm glad you came." Smiling.

"How are they treating you?" Searching his face, his eyes following her caressive glance. "You look good, rested."

"Sweet." Harvie laughing.

"You know what I mean?"

"I know. Let me touch you." Sticking his forefinger through a laced pore in the wire partition between them. Nellie touching his forefinger; Harvie wrapping his finger around hers. "Sweet. How are you doing? You look like you can use some rest."

"I'm worried sick that they'll execute you or something. You didn't do it, Harvie. Why did you say you did a terrible thing like that when you didn't do it?"

"I guess I wanted to do something with my life—"

"You mean give it away? Is that what you wanted to do—give your life away?"

"It didn't mean anything to me the way it was. I wanted it to mean something. I needed to make something happen. I wanted to break out of myself. My life wasn't real to me. I was desperate. I had to be locked up. I had to come to myself."

"But did you have to go this far, say you killed somebody? If they execute you, I'll die, too."

"I won't be executed. Don't worry. You're not wearing make-up. Why not?"

"I guess I forgot." Knowing that she left it off because she didn't want to look too cheerful, too bright with Harvie shut away from cheerfulness, from brightness. Seeing that it would have been all right after all, Harvie looking well.

"And that dress. It doesn't even look like you, Nellie. You don't have to look plain for me. Beauty doesn't offend me. You'll make me think that you've already started mourning me."

"Harvie, please don't tease me like that."

"Then wear that yellow dress the next time you come."

"I will, Harvie. Are they treating you all right? Do they feed you enough? What do you do all day?"

"They treat me all right. They don't give me those delicious steaks you cook for me, but they feed me. I work in the stone quarry."

"Stone quarry? That's a laborer's work."

"It's what I want to do, Nellie."

"But you never did that kind of work. You're not used to it."

"I'm getting used to it. I found my work, Nellie. The feeling of satisfaction I get when I'm standing among the stone knowing I can move it. Did you know that there's water underneath the stone?"

"Water?"

"There is. I'll show you sometime when I'm free. I'll show you what I learned. I'll take you to work with me and you can watch your Harvie move the earth."

"I'll want to see, Harvie. I'll want to see whatever you do. I'll want to share it. Harvie—I went to a dance the other night. I wanted to get my mind from you; but they kept playing that music we used to listen to together. Remember? Before you got so restless?"

Eyes searching.

"I remember." Tightening his forefinger around hers.

"Every time a man asked me to dance I wanted to cry because it wasn't you, because I couldn't dance with the rhythm I feel for you. I wanted to feel everything, but only with you. I'm mad for you, Harvie."

"Don't make it hard for me, Nellie. You love me too much."

"How can I love you too much?"

"You can, Nellie. You can."

"You're trying to prepare me for something. What are you trying to prepare me for? I don't want to possess you. All I want is to love you. You possess *me*."

"I don't want you to love me too much. If I have to go away—"

"Why would you go away?"

"If I should—I may just want to pick up and go away. I'd want to feel free to go. And I want you to feel free, too. You won't be free if you love me too much. I feel I have a second chance to life, Nellie. I'll not hold back on it. You're different, it's hard for you to understand."

"You keep saying that to me. What is there that is so special to your life that I can't experience? I have to control my feelings, and you're free to satisfy yours. That's the only difference. I understand your feelings or I wouldn't be here now."

"Sweet Nellie. How much I must make you suffer. I don't mean to."

"I know you don't mean to."

"I'm building a monument in the workshop."

"Do you mean sculpture?"

"I guess you can call it that. It's going to be called 'The Workers.' And after that I'm going to build a monument to you."

"Harvie."

"I know exactly what I'm going to do. I've started working on 'The Workers.' I want to finish it before the trial. In case I don't go free, you can see it gets a fitting place. My hands feel liberated even if I don't get free, as long as they put me where I can work with my hands."

"You'll be free, Harvie. You said so. That lawyer, Mr. London, is good. Isn't he? He'll get you free. Harvie, I think it's time to go. What will I do?"

"You'll go, sweet. Wait—let me touch more of you," sticking all of his fingers through the laced pores in the wired separation between them, she doing the same. Locking their fingers together.

"That feels good. Now go. Hurry before they lock you in."

"Harvie, I wish they would. I'm so mad for you—"

"You foolish woman." Watching her hurry away, turning away himself.

Harvie Guthrie sitting in the courtroom staring at the life-size stone sculpture of a man and a woman; the man, in shirt sleeves rolled to his elbows, is cast gripping a hammer above his head, the other hand pressing a chisel against a large chunk of stone held in place by the huge palm of the woman beside him. All eyes which see it bear witness to this creation titled 'The Workers' carved by Harvie's hands. A tribute and a penance.

Harvie turning from the sculpture, his stare broken by his awareness of the sudden hush in the courtroom. Sweat raining from his armpits. The prosecutor is about to make his closing statement to the jury.

"Ladies and gentlemen of the jury. Punish Harvie Guthrie. Swiftly and firmly. Deal with him while you have him."

Harvie feeling pressure bearing upon his brain, his chest; feeling his body grow taut, though his hands feel liberated.

Nellie sitting in the row of seats behind Harvie, her yellow dress as much a part of the dress rehearsal as the smile waiting for Harvie should he look her way.

Hardy Gallant listening to the prosecutor's last words.

". . . We ask you to bring in a verdict that the defendant is guilty of murder in the first degree."

Starting from his stare, sweat pricking his forehead. "But I didn't—"

The judge's gavel reigning. Mr. Guthrie, control yourself. "Will the defense make his closing statement to the jury?"

Hardy Gallant, born Carl London, rising from his chair, brushing a black wave of hair from his forehead, walking slowly toward the jury, twisting his shoulders in his new suit.

"Ladies and gentlemen of the jury, you don't mind if I liberate myself from this coat, do you? You know how it is. You're all hard workers who have taken time from regular jobs to set a man free. Now, you men know what it means to get out of a coat and roll up your sleeves. You feel liberated, free to get at the depth of the job." Taking off his coat, draping it over the railing enclosing the jury, rolling up his sleeves. "You gentlemen can take your jackets off. That's right, just put them over the back of your chair. Good, don't we all feel like men, liberated? We're in touch. Now, you ladies, you can take off your shoes. Don't laugh. I know a bit about pinched toes. When your feet are free, you feel good all over. Now you take a deep breath. Don't you feel liberated? Now *don't* you? You're laughing; but doesn't it feel good to be liberated? We're in touch.

"Ladies and gentlemen of the jury, you're a responsible group of people. That is why you were chosen to liberate that man, Harvie Guthrie, from the charge of murder.

"Yet at the same time this is not a murder trial. The murderer of Gertrude Swank is not in this room. This is not a murder trial. Harvie Gurthrie, the man, is not on trial. Rather, the truth of life is on trial. The good life, the meaningful life, the fulfilled life. What is a man if he cannot fulfill his life; what, indeed, is a woman if she cannot fulfill her life? They are but the living dead. They are those for whom living has been in vain. This is what Harvie Guthrie was fighting—a life in vain. His life. Harvie Guthrie is a vital man in every vein, muscle, tendon. He felt his own life was passing him. He felt caught in the rush of men rushing for the moon, computers competing with his brain, machines defying his hands, hearts changing bodies, old societies dissolving and new societies emerging, while he remained caught in the vortex.

"So when he read that Gertrude Swank was dead—and that the murderer was still at large—he saw a chance to give his life meaning, to give his life momentum by laying it in jeopardy, by confessing to a murder that he did not commit." Pausing, looking from one jury member to the other.

"A murderer is not on trial here. The death of Gertrude Swank is not the issue. Life is the issue. This is a trial against the mechanical life, against the superficial life, against the static life.

This is not a courtroom in the technical sense. This is a forum for a man who sought meaning, fulfillment of his life even in these times of murder and creation, of technology outdistancing human assimilation." Rolling his sleeves above his elbows.

"Do you wonder, then, that Harvie Guthrie should feel caught? Do you wonder why he should have risked losing his life in order to get a firmer grasp on it?" Seizing the railing, the structure cracking, the wooden support tumbling to the floor, two jurymen rising from their seats to give assistance. Hardy Gallant gesturing to them to remain seated, letting the wood fall from his hands to the floor. "It is only a piece of wood. I can pay the cost of wood. But who among you is so firm that he would not be moved to admit that it is difficult to live a natural life today? Who among you is so firm that he has not been moved to question his own life? Who among you is so positive that he has not questioned the meaning of his work, of his accomplishments—or lack of accomplishments?

"Look at the sculpture: Exhibit Life. It's called 'The Workers' and it was created by Harvie Guthrie, the man whom you have come to liberate, in the prison workshop as a kind of penance and tribute to you and to all of the workers.

"It is made of stone which he helped quarry from the earth. Notice the weary but strong face of the woman. Surely she is the reflection of Gertrude Swank, of all women workers to whom Harvie Guthrie pays tribute. Notice the man strong and determined, a hammer in one hand and a chisel in the other, sleeves rolled up, eyes steady upon what he is doing.

"Do you not see your reflection; do you not see the reflection of the late Gertrude Swank, for whose death it is said that Harvie Guthrie stands to answer to you? Not so. You have not come here to condemn. You have come to witness truth, the truth of our dilemma. Do you not see the reflection of yourselves, of Gertrude Swank holding in place the stone into which the man is driving his chisel? Of course, you do, because you're in touch with life and reality.

"Harvie Guthrie, the man who presented himself to you in the first place, has created this monument of blood, sinew, and courage as his tribute to Gertrude Swank and to you. He has worked hard and well. What indeed men have to say to one another they say through their good works. What, indeed, men feel for one another they express by reaching out to take a hand—not to take a life. Indeed, what use can one man gain from another man's life which he has taken or caused to be taken if that life has ceased?

"Harvie Guthrie is a man of good works. He is a man afire, burning to create good works. Surely you will allow no one to put out his fire. You put forth too great an appearance for that. You are too strong on the side of justice. Where are the prime movers who build on what is good? There is Harvie Guthrie and there are you.

"We are never at a loss for judges and jurors—but *prime movers,* the men and women who responsibly create, why there's a crop we have not enough of. True, Gertrude Swank is dead, was murdered by a person or persons not yet apprehended. But her life was unjust. So we murder injustice and create justice which is responsible and which considers everyone.

"Harvie has some violence in him, of course. What man of blood and sinew does not? And he used it upon himself in that he constantly ripped his insides apart in an effort to break out of himself and claim his true work. He has some violence in him, of course. Ask his love, Nellie, who responded to his violent love-making with love and understanding. Ask Nellie about the powerful hands of Harvie Guthrie, those restless hands that sought appeasement in her warmth, hands that created 'The Workers,' hands whose only violence erupted upon the keys of an adding machine day after day. This man with so much creative potential in his hands, hands whose only violence on the night of the murder of Gertrude Swank was to batter a windowpane in the apartment of Nellie Worth, his love. Afterwards, she rocked him to sleep in her arms.

"Oh, you know how it is. You're in touch. Indeed you are. What we have to say to each other we say through our understanding and our love.

"Were Harvie Guthrie a man other than the man he is—

creator, worker, lover of humanity and human beings—he *might* have murdered Gertrude Swank. But, of course, you know that he did not murder Gertrude Swank. Instead, he seized upon the sensation of the murder of Gertrude Swank, and having already been provided with newspaper accounts of the tragedy, confessed to her murder to gain a response to his own static existence, to the meaninglessness of his life, to his own torment, to his inner cries for help.

"He equated Gertrude Swank's colorless life with the colorlessness of his own. An innocent man would not confess guilt unless he was desperate for life; unless he was making a desperate appeal to life to acknowledge him, to give him a second chance, and to compensate him in the second chance for omitting him from meaningful participation in the first.

"Surely you understand his dilemma. That is why you are here —to help Harvie Guthrie gain a second chance.

"Look at his fine piece of creation. He worked on it for months with hammer and chisel, waiting for you to come forth to hear him out. Ladies and gentlemen, notice Harvie Guthrie, fine young man, full of life and purpose. Surely you will not interrupt his life now that he has truthfully found his purpose.

"Look at that fine young man with calloused hands. He got those callouses creating his fine tribute to Gertrude Swank and to you—his fine tribute to 'The Workers.' Notice this young man whose Nellie is waiting for him in this courtroom, waiting for your voice to fortify his liberation and yours.

"Who among you is so firm that he cannot be moved to see the truth? There he is, sitting there. The truth of you and me. And truth would murder no one.

"Do your appointed work. Shout 'Not guilty!'

"For what, indeed, men communicate to one another, they communicate through their good works—forever."

ABOUT THE AUTHOR

AUDREY LEE's first novel, *The Clarion People,* was published
by McGraw-Hill in 1968. Catherine Marshall has called her
"a new novelist of rich promise." Miss Lee lives in Philadelphia.
She is currently at work on her third novel.